THE DAYSTAR VOYAGES

SECRET OF THE PLANET MAKON

GILBERT MORRIS
AND DAN MEEKS

MOODY PRESS
CHICAGO

Moody Press, a ministry of the Moody Bible Institute,
is designed for education, evangelization, and edification.
If we may assist you in knowing more about Christ
and the Christian life, please write us without obligation:
Moody Press, c/o MLM, Chicago, Illinois 60610.

All Scripture quotations, unless indicated, are taken from the *New
American Standard Bible*, © 1960, 1962, 1963, 1968, 1971, 1972, 1973,
1975, 1977, and 1994 by The Lockman Foundation, La Habra, Calif. Used
by permission.

ISBN: 0-8024-4105-X

5 7 9 10 8 6

Printed in the United States of America

To Gilbert and Johnnie Morris—from Danny

You have been an "Aquila and Priscilla" in so many lives. I count myself most blessed to be included in that number. I thank you from the bottom of my heart for taking the time to explain the way of God to me more perfectly. I have no one else like you. I love you very much!

Contents

1. Jerusha Gets an Offer   7
2. Crew of the *Daystar*   19
3. The Ensigns   31
4. The Navigator   43
5. Six Babies, a Mutt, and a Grandma   53
6. The Shadow   65
7. A Traitor Unmasked   75
8. Dai Bando Takes a Stand   91
9. Ringo Fails the Test   101
10. Antigravity   115
11. A Loving God   127
12. Chief Locar   135
13. A Kiss from Captain Edge   145
14. Attack!   155
15. A New Commission   165

1
Jerusha Gets an Offer

A sense of humiliation came over Jerusha Ericson, and she felt tears begin to sting her eyes. Quickly she blinked, determined not to show any sign of weakness before the commander of the Intergalactic Academy. She blinked furiously and then looked across the ebony desk at Commander Marta Inch.

"I'm sorry to have to give you this news," Commander Inch said, "but you have left me no other choice, Ensign."

Commander Inch was a short woman with iron gray hair and steely gray eyes. She sat scrutinizing the girl, who stood at attention, wearing the maroon tunic that marked an ensign of the Academy. "We have given you every chance to succeed here at the Academy, but I'm afraid that you are too . . . innovative."

Although the commander chose her words carefully and was an expert at hiding her feelings, Jerusha knew exactly what was going on in the officer's mind. Jerusha had found she could sense emotions almost as keenly as most people sensed a breeze or a peculiar smell—and the smell that came from Commander Marta Inch was that of antagonism amounting close to hatred.

Jerusha had known for a long time that the head of the Academy despised her, but she had not thought she would be expelled. Now, however, she saw that the situation was hopeless. Straightening her back, she said, "Will that be all, Commander?"

Commander Inch seemed somewhat taken aback by the young ensign who answered her so directly. What she saw was a girl of fifteen with ash-blonde hair and intensely dark blue eyes set in a squarish face. She was tall for a girl, at least five ten, and perhaps the fact that she was also very attractive had something to do with Commander Inch's dislike. The commander was not attractive by anyone's standards.

She said sternly, "The committee regrets having to take this action, Ensign. If you will tender an apology and modify your behavior . . ."

"What have I done that was wrong, Commander?"

"Wrong? Your whole attitude has been wrong since the day you came here!" Commander Inch snapped, her gray eyes turning cold as polar ice. "You are a rebel, and that's the kindest way I can put it! We have no room for your sort here, but if you're willing to apologize to me and to the rest of the staff and to accept the discipline we will hand down—and give me your word that there will be no more of your rebellious ways—"

"Thank you, Commander. I will not be staying at the Academy."

Jerusha turned and walked stiffly out of the room, her head high and her lips tight. She knew that Commander Inch was glaring, and she heard her say, "Just a minute—" But she slammed the door behind her and walked past the adjutant, who stared at her with shock. No one *ever* slammed the door on Commander Inch!

Leaving the offices of the commanding officer, Jerusha strode down the hallway. Large panes of glass allowed beams of yellow sunlight to enter, illuminating the walkway that led to the main part of the Academy, where most of the training took place. She took the elevator to the ground floor. Stepping out, she heard her name called and turned to face two of her fellow ensigns, who came toward her.

"Well, did you smooth it over with the commander?"

The speaker was a tall boy of approximately sixteen named Karl Bentlow. He was handsome, had blond wavy hair, and fancied himself a ladies' man. His charms had failed with Jerusha, however, and there was a hidden smile in his eyes as if he knew what had happened.

"No, I didn't smooth it over," Jerusha said. "I'm leaving."

"Oh, that's too bad!" Olga Von Kemp was short with dark hair and darker eyes. She had a masculine manner and a domineering attitude that had brought her into conflict with Jerusha many times. Now she tried to give Jerusha what she probably felt was a sympathetic look, but failed. "I'll be glad to speak to Commander Inch if you want to stay, Jerusha."

"I wouldn't stay here—" Jerusha gritted her teeth "—if they would give me the whole Academy!"

Karl said, "Now wait a minute, Jerusha! You're making a mistake. If you'd just learn to bend a little bit—"

"Worms bend, Karl!" Jerusha spoke quietly, but then saw it was useless.

Karl and Olga headed a group at the Intergalactic Academy that formed a sort of club among the younger cadets. They were the elite students among the younger group, and both had been insulted when Jerusha failed to surrender to their domineering leadership.

Now Jerusha said briefly, "This is good-bye. I won't be seeing you again." She turned and walked away.

"Well, I'm glad *she's* leaving!" Karl snapped. He looked angrily after the tall blonde-haired girl. "She's a stuck-up spoiled brat and has to have her own way!"

9

Olga smiled slightly, for she knew Karl very well. "Your charms didn't work too well on her, did they?" She knew this would upset him because his pride had been bruised. Taking his arm, she said, "It's better that she's leaving." Her voice was filled with satisfaction, and her dark eyes gleamed with pleasure. She had disliked Jerusha intensely, and she thought with satisfaction, *Now, Karl, you won't be chasing after that blonde iceberg.*

But aloud she said, "Come along. Let's go to class."

Jerusha had kept her composure in front of Commander Inch and had shown no weakness in front of Karl and Olga. She continued to maintain a straight face as she rode a traveling sidewalk through town, for she wanted no one to see any weakness in her. She carried a small suitcase, which contained all of her belongings.

Eventually she left the moving sidewalk and wound her way into the outer part of the city. In the old days the section would have been called a "slum." The word had passed out of use long ago; nevertheless, it described the area perfectly.

Jerusha went by buildings that had begun to decay. More than once, sinister shadowy figures came toward her. But she turned them away with a curt word and finally arrived at the narrow twisting street where she had found a room. She looked with distaste at the building. It had the single word *Rooms* over the doorway, and she moved with resignation toward it.

The twilight was deepening, and she was alone. Suddenly, despite herself, tears rose in her eyes and ran down her cheeks. Jerusha stopped abruptly. She had not wept for years, not since she was a child. But losing her place as an ensign at the Intergalactic Academy was the worst blow she had ever gotten.

Standing before the shabby rooming house, she remembered how proud she had been when the news came that she was accepted. When she had donned her uniform for the first time, her heart had seemed to glow within her. And she knew she had done well at the Academy. She had been one of the brightest students there. But she thought now of how she had crossed Commander Inch and other officers by what they called her "rebelliousness."

"I didn't *mean* to seem rebellious," she muttered. "But there's no help for it now. I'll just have to find something else." She walked toward the doorway, depressed, not even wiping the tears from her cheeks. She had no plans at all. When it became obvious that she was going to be expelled, she had found a room in this dilapidated part of town, and now it would be her home.

"Just a minute—"

Jerusha was taken off guard. The darkness had grown more dense than she'd realized, and the tall man who emerged suddenly out of the gloom brought her a start of alarm. This was a rough part of town, and the man could be dangerous!

She turned to face him squarely, dropping the suitcase and automatically going into a defensive position, her hands extended so that the hard edges of her palms could be used as a weapon. She was an expert at the old martial arts, but the shadowy figure that emerged looked fit and able.

"Get away from me!" Jerusha said quietly.

The man stopped abruptly. "No trouble. I just want to talk to you."

"I'll bet you do! Go away and leave me alone!"

By the dim light that partly illuminated the murky street, she saw that he was young. She guessed his age at around twenty-five. He had an athletic build, was broad shouldered and slim hipped. He wore a nondescript gray jacket, a pair of tightfitting black trousers, and half boots. The hat shoved back on his head was flat crowned, and from under it light curls escaped.

He stood watching her intently. "I don't mean you any harm. Truly." His voice was rather pleasant. "I've been waiting for you."

"I don't know you."

"No, but I know you."

"I've never seen you before in my life. Now, go away and leave me alone!"

The man made a bad mistake then. He took a step forward, and as he did, Jerusha's right hand moved so fast that it blurred. The hard edge of her palm struck him in the throat, which brought a strangled gasp. However, he fended off her next blow and took her arm, saying in a raspy whisper, "Wait a minute! I just want—"

He had no time to finish what he had started to say, for out of the thickening darkness the shadowy form of a very large dog appeared. The man only had time to hear the low growl and turn to see the animal hurtling through the air.

"Wait!" he called out, but the dog struck him in the chest and catapulted him backwards. He put out his hands vainly to shove the dog away. "Get this thing off me! He's going to bite my face off!"

"Hold him, Contessa!"

Jerusha took a deep breath and felt a moment's gratitude for her dog. Any man who could take a blow in the throat from an expert in martial arts would not be easy to stop. She placed her hand on the neck of the huge animal, which had both front paws planted on the fallen man's chest and was growling deep in her throat. "All right, Contessa. Let him up."

The German shepherd at once backed away but kept her eyes fixed on the man as he crawled to his feet. "Now will you go away, or do I need to have Contessa encourage you?"

Slowly the man stood, giving the dog a cautious look. "You know," he said in a conversational tone, "I'm not really afraid of most things, but somehow big dogs have always made me nervous."

"Go away and you won't be nervous!"

The man picked up his hat and shoved it on his head. "My name is Captain Mark Edge, and you're Jerusha Ericson."

Jerusha was shocked that he knew her name. At first she thought he was someone sent from the Academy for some reason, but he did not have the trim Academy look nor did he wear the uniform.

"How do you know my name?"

"I've asked around about you," the man called Edge said.

He began to say more, and Jerusha paid less attention to the words that he said than she did to what she sensed in him. It was a way she had. She could not explain it. She was just hypersensitive.

She stood quietly listening to Captain Edge, her eyes fixed on him. *He's not dangerous*, she decided. *He's hiding something, and he's got some sort of fear—but he means no harm.* Reassured, she said, "All right. Come on in."

Edge smiled then. He had a wedge-shaped face with a wide mouth, and Jerusha noticed that he had a very nice smile.

As they stepped inside, she touched the switch, and he blinked at the sudden light. Looking around the apartment—one room, a bath, and a miniature kitchen —he said, "Pretty crummy place, isn't it?"

Jerusha glared. "Pretty crummy," she agreed. "Did you come here to talk about the crummy room I have?"

"No." Mark Edge turned toward her. "I've come to ask you to join a crew I'm putting together."

Jerusha stared at him, speechless. She had expected anything but this. Ever since she had been aware that she was going to be expelled, she had tried to think of what to do next, and she had not a clue to this point. Again she sensed the honesty of this man, but still there was something secretive, something perhaps he was blocking out even in his own mind.

"Are you recruiting people who have been kicked out of the Intergalactic Academy?"

Edge's grin grew broader. "So they did kick you out. I heard that's the way it would be."

"Where did you hear that?"

Edge shrugged. "These things get around. But what I want—" He broke off, suddenly startled, looked down, and his smile left. "Would you mind asking the dog to go somewhere else?"

Then Jerusha recognized that the fear she had sensed in him was of the dog. It was not a tremendous fear, but she enjoyed seeing his discomfort. She looked down at the German shepherd, who was pushing against Edge's legs. Suddenly the animal reached up and licked his hand.

"She likes you." Jerusha smiled, enjoying the look on his face.

Captain Edge shifted his feet uncomfortably. "Well," he said, giving an apprehensive look at the huge beast, "they say you can always trust a man that dogs like."

"That's nonsense," Jerusha said. "I've known absolute villains that dogs love. Now, what do you want, Edge, or is it Captain Edge? Captain of what?" she demanded.

14

"Well, this is going to take a little time. Do you suppose we could sit down?"

"I suppose so." Jerusha looked with distaste about the room. There were only two chairs, and both looked rickety. "Sit down there, if you wish. I'm sorry I don't have anything to offer you."

"No problem." Edge sat down, and to his dismay the dog rose and put both forefeet on his lap. She leaned forward and growled, but it was a pleasant growl. Before he could move, she licked his face. "Hey, stop that!"

Jerusha sat watching his ineffectual efforts to shove Contessa away. She felt very comfortable with the man now. "Don't you like dogs?"

"No, I can't stand them. Get her off me, will you?"

"Sit down, Contessa. Leave him alone." Jerusha watched the dog reluctantly move away.

Contessa did not go far, however, but sat down and looked up soulfully at Captain Edge's face. Her behavior puzzled Jerusha, for Contessa was a one-woman dog—up until now. She tried to pick up more of the emotions that came from this tall man who sat stiffly before her, eyeing the dog. But it was confusing.

"All right. Let's hear your story. You know I've been expelled, but do you know why?"

Edge leaned back and turned his eyes to Jerusha's face. "If the rumor I heard was true, you're too rebellious for the Academy. Is that right?"

Jerusha ignored his question. "Tell me about this crew that you're recruiting."

For a long moment the two looked at each other. Perhaps Edge was trying to figure out how best to tell his story. He said, "I've got a strange story to tell you. I'll make it brief."

"Good."

Edge grinned at the sharpness of her tone. "You've got a pretty abrupt manner. All right, here's the story. There's a planet called Makon out there in the galaxy. Not many people know where it is, and I hope nobody finds out. I was serving as captain of a ship doing some exploratory work for—well, I'll leave out his name."

"You might as well tell me. I'll find out sooner or later."

"Probably so," Captain Edge said reluctantly. "Well, you know this name, I guess—Sir Richard Irons."

Despite herself, Jerusha's eyes flew open. Everybody knew Sir Richard Irons. He was a ruthless man of great wealth and power, little more than a space pirate if what she had heard was true. "That's not much recommendation—if you're working for a pirate like Irons."

A grin creased the captain's tanned face. "My sentiments exactly. Anyway, I found this planet while I was out on a jaunt on my own. And while there, I discovered it has one thing that would be very interesting to anyone who would like to be rich and powerful."

"And what's that, Captain Edge?"

"A gem called tridium. Harder than diamonds, Ensign. Do you know what that means?"

Jerusha well knew what that meant. The world had once had many diamonds for industrial use, but these had been consumed from Earth's surface, and now there was a tremendous search for other diamonds or a diamond substitute. If what Edge said was true, the man or woman who controlled a diamond substitute would indeed be rich and powerful.

"Where is this planet?"

Edge smiled again, which caused the dog to whine and rise and try to put her paw on his knee.

Edge said, "I'm not telling, but I'm going back there."

"Under Sir Richard Irons's contract?"

"No. But I've got to go back and get a sample or two. That's all it'll take."

"So do you have a ship?"

"I have a ship, but I'm short on crew. That's why I've come to you. If what I hear is true, you're an engineering genius and a flight engineer."

"I can handle that, but I'll have to know more than you've told me so far."

"All right. We'll have to trust each other." Edge stood to his feet. "If you'll come, I'll show you the ship and introduce you to the crew I've got already. Then we can talk some more."

Jerusha had no other plans. She did not hesitate. "All right, Captain Edge. We'll go take a look at this ship of yours."

2
Crew of the *Daystar*

The journey by electrocar from Jerusha's apartment to the destination Mark Edge had in mind was confusing to her. The captain took them down several twisting streets and then said, "I'm sorry, but I'll have to blindfold you at this point."

Jerusha looked suspiciously at the tall man beside her. "What for?" she demanded.

Edge drummed his fingers on the dashboard of the electrocar. "I've become a very cautious man in the last few weeks, Miss Ericson," he admitted finally. His eyes darted rapidly over the buildings that lined the street in front of them. Then he turned back to Jerusha. "I know this sounds like a very bad novel, but I'm really apprehensive about my ship being found."

"Found by whom?"

"We don't have time to go into that. Will you let me blindfold you, or shall I take you back to your room?"

For just one instant Jerusha hesitated. She thought, *I don't like this. There's something going on in his mind that he doesn't want me to know. But I've got no other job to go to, so I might as well see this out.* Shrugging, she said, "All right. Go ahead with the blindfold."

She sat stiffly while Edge pulled a silk neckerchief from his pocket and tied it around her eyes. "That too tight?" he asked.

"No, it's fine."

"All right. Here we go."

Jerusha tried to keep track of the turns, but it was

impossible. She knew that she would never be able to find her way back again.

Then the electrocar hissed to a stop, and she felt Edge's hand fumbling at the knot behind her hair.

"I'll do it," she said briskly.

When the blindfold was removed, she saw that they were parked inside some sort of large, empty building. Pillars held it up, and only a few glimmering solar lights burned feebly to illuminate the scene. "Well, where's the ship?" she demanded.

Edge got out, and when she joined him, he nodded toward a set of double doors over to his left. "It's right in there," he said. He paused, then said, "I hope you're not expecting too much."

"What do you mean?"

"Well, you've been at the Intergalactic Academy training on state-of-the-art P54 Combat Corsairs, not to mention the Magnum Deep Space Cruisers. My ship isn't as fancy and is just a little bit older than what you're used to."

Jerusha pondered that as she walked by his side. He had long legs, and she had to hurry to keep up, which irritated her. When he reached the doors, he put his hand over a glass plate and grinned at her. "A print lock," he said. "Works on my fingerprints alone."

"I know about those," Jerusha said with some annoyance. He had spoken to her as if she were a child, and she resented that.

Suddenly the doors slid open noiselessly. She saw a very large hangar, and in the middle of it sat a spaceship.

"Is *that* it?"

"I told you not to be expecting too much!" Edge's voice was testy. "This isn't exactly the Intergalactic Academy!"

"It certainly isn't!" Jerusha was shocked by the sight of the ship but was curious nevertheless. "What in the world is it? I've never seen anything quite like it."

"There isn't anything 'quite like it.'" Pride filled his eyes, and he smiled fondly as they approached the cruiser. "You'll like it better after you get used to it."

"Captain, you've got to do something about the phase inhibitors," a voice said. "This new design overstresses them. They're as old as the ones we just replaced. I can't adjust the intermix on the Star Drive properly. Also, the wing struts have to be reinforced— the extra thrust will shear them apart."

Jerusha looked around to see a short, thickset man wearing a pair of dirty white coveralls. He was no more than four and a half feet tall but was perfectly proportioned. He had brown eyes and thick brown hair that curled rebelliously. And then he turned his sharp-featured face toward her. Cocking his head to one side, he looked up at her, then transferred his glance to the captain. "Who is *this?*"

"She may be your new assistant, Ivan. This is Jerusha Ericson. Jerusha, Ivan Petroski, chief engineer."

Petroski's lips pulled down in a frown. He shook his head violently. "She won't do! She's just a child!"

"Wait until you try me before you say that." Jerusha was half angered and half amused by the small man. "When you grow up," she added, "I may listen to you a little bit more."

"He *is* grown up," Captain Edge said quickly. "He comes from the planet Bellinka. Everyone there is about his size."

"No!" Petroski snapped shortly. "I was the *tallest* man in my tribe, and if you think size is the measure of an individual, maybe I'll have to show you a thing or two!" He stepped forward, willing right then to engage in a brawl.

He was stopped by Edge's voice. "We don't have time for this, Lieutenant. After I show our guest around, you may want to tell her a little bit more about the engineering features of the ship."

"I'll be glad to hear it," Jerusha said. She was thinking quickly, *If this is going to be my superior, I'd better not get his back up.* "I'm sorry I spoke so rudely," she said. "There was no excuse for that." She tried to sense what the dwarf was feeling. She decided that, though there was anger in him, there was nothing really violent or threatening.

Petroski stared hard at her. "We'll see!" he muttered, then wheeled and walked away.

"He's a little grumpy but a fine engineer," Edge said. "Now, let me tell you about the ship. Do you remember much of your space flight history lessons?"

Looking intently at the spacecraft, Jerusha nodded her head. "I've a good memory of everything that I've ever studied, including space flight history, but I've never seen this type of ship before. My best guess is that it is a failed prototype and you probably won it while gambling. I can't believe this thing will fly!"

"As a matter of fact, I did win the aft section but not at gambling. And it does fly. How do you think I got it here?"

Jerusha circled to the rear of the ship, giving it a closer examination. "How'd you win it, then?" she asked as she reached the aft thrusters.

"I placed tenth in a plasma jet race." Edge slapped the aft wing with his hand. "This was the booby prize. My former boss got a big laugh out of it."

Jerusha's eyebrows lifted when she came to the main fuselage section. "This looks vaguely familiar."

Edge walked up beside her. "This is the heart of the ship. It was manufactured by the Klueken Space Corporation about fifty years ago."

Jerusha exclaimed, "This is an old Klueken Starthruster?"

Edge laughed as he watched the former academy student piece together his ship in her mind. "Fancy name for a freighter, don't you think?" he asked her.

"Well," Jerusha answered, "it looks more like a Starthruster now than it did then. You've really done a remarkable job, Captain. The main fuselage is from a Klueken freighter, the aft section wings and Star Drive must be from a Viprex cruiser, and the forward sensor array appears to be Dorisian."

"Very, very good! I had a feeling about you. It takes a really good engineer to recognize what I've put together here." Edge's voice swelled with pride. "Once we reinstall the forward stabilizers and thrusters, she should be ready to go. I call her the *Daystar*. What do you think?"

Actually, Jerusha was impressed. The ship was rough-looking and crude in many ways, but it was obvious that Edge was himself an engineer with a fine mind—and a fine hand for creating. *Anyone who could make a ship out of spare parts like this*, she thought, *I'll have to give him credit*. "I'll have to see the ship in action," she said aloud.

"Well, you'll see that if you decide to come with us. Now I want you to meet some of the other crew members."

The next crew member that they met was rather intimidating. "This is Tara Jaleel, our weapons officer."

The woman who turned to stare at Jerusha was more than six feet tall. Her skin was black as ebony, and her features, though attractive, had a fierce quality about them. She listened impassively as Captain Edge explained why he had brought the visitor, then she nodded slightly, not offering her hand. "Do you have courage?" she demanded.

Jerusha, who had been attempting her usual mood reading on the weapons officer, was taken aback at the question. "I suppose I have as much as is necessary."

Lieutenant Jaleel's generous lips turned up into a smile. "If you stay, I will, perhaps, test you out on that."

As they walked away, Edge said quietly, "Did you ever hear of the Masai?"

"I don't think so."

"They were a very fierce tribe of warriors back on Earth years ago. They were the most feared fighters on the African continent, afraid of nothing. They lived to fight." He grimaced and said, "I'm afraid Lieutenant Jaleel is a little *too* aggressive."

"Well, aggressiveness may not be a *bad* thing in a weapons officer, Captain."

"No, but be careful. She's an expert at martial arts." He moved his shoulder carefully. "She enticed me into a bout with her a few days ago, and I'm still sore all over. She's quick as a snake and stronger than you would believe a woman could be. Very dangerous. But as you say, this is what a weapons officer should be. There is our communications officer."

Edge led Jerusha to one of the strangest-looking men she had ever seen.

"This is Zeno Thrax, our communications officer. Commander Thrax, this is a candidate for our crew, Miss Jerusha Ericson."

"I'm very happy to know you." Thrax was a perfect albino. He had pure white hair, eyes of no color at all but, rather, pale and chilling to look at. He wore a black uniform, and the blackness emphasized his colorless features and hair. He took in Jerusha at one glance.

"Where are you from, Lieutenant?"

"I come from Mentor Seven."

"I don't believe I know that one."

"I'm afraid you wouldn't like it."

"Why not?"

"Because nothing can live on the surface. Everyone on my planet lives underground."

"Some fine mines on Mentor Seven," Edge remarked.

"True," the albino said. "Everyone there is a miner."

It occurred to Jerusha that Zeno Thrax seemed a lonely man. *Why, I believe he would like to go back to his people,* she thought. *I wonder why he can't go back.*

Thrax said, "I can never go back to my home again." It was as though he had read her thoughts, which, of course, he hadn't, but— He turned abruptly and left the two standing there.

"Why can't he go back to his home?"

"Nobody knows." Edge shrugged. "He doesn't talk about it. I think he violated some taboo among his people and has been exiled for life. A very sad man. You'd never know it, but he has a wry sense of humor, and he loves games of any kind. A fine communications officer too."

Jerusha frowned. "Is he a mind reader?"

"I think you'll find Thrax to be quite a normal human being—but sometimes he does surprise me by picking up on what I'm thinking. He's a smart fellow, no question about it."

"Well—" Jerusha looked up at the cruiser once again—"I think it's time you told me a little bit more about this project of yours, Captain."

"Very well. We'll go into my cabin."

Jerusha followed the captain as he circled the ship and then spoke to a door. "Open!" he commanded.

The door swung back, and she said, "Voice lock?"

"That's right. Come inside."

His quarters were hardly more ornate than her own. It was a plain, simple room with a bunk bed on one side, cabinet-refrigerator and bookcases on the other, and a desk cluttered with papers.

"You'll have to excuse this place. I don't spend much time here. Just sleeping mostly. Have a seat. How about something to drink?"

"All right."

Edge went over to the cabinet and took out two glasses. Then he removed a bottle from the refrigerator. It contained a white liquid. "Try this."

Jerusha took a sip cautiously, and then her eyes opened wide. "What *is* this?"

"Real fresh milk."

"It doesn't taste like milk."

"That's because you've only had artificial powdered stuff. This came from a real cow."

"A *cow?* Where did you ever get a cow?"

Edge sipped his milk, and it left a mustache on his upper lip. He grinned, and his teeth looked white against his tanned skin. "Oh, I have my methods. Nothing like fresh milk. Of course, we can't take a cow into space."

Jerusha drank the milk. Most food was processed these days and could be very unappetizing. One of the things she enjoyed was having fresh fruits and vegetables, which were difficult to get. She savored the milk and then put down the glass. "All right. What about this planet that we're going to find?"

"I've already told you most of it," Edge said. "I found this planet when I was out on patrol, exploring, and discovered that it's uncharted. I also discovered that it's got tridium."

"I never heard of tridium."

"Of course you haven't." Edge laughed. "I made up the name myself. All I know is, it's harder than diamonds."

"Are they just scattered on the surface? You just reach down and pick them up?"

"Nothing like that," Edge said. "Tridium has to be mined."

Something about the captain's attitude disturbed Jerusha. *He's hiding something. He's telling most of the truth, but not all of it.* Finally she said, "If I'm going to go join your crew, I'll have to know more than you've told me. What are you keeping back?"

Edge did not seem surprised. "I was afraid you'd find me out, perceptive as you are." He put his hands on the table and clasped them together. He had broad hands, and the fingers were long and strong-looking. "Well, I might as well let you know the worst. I stole the Mark V Star Drive, and if I get caught I'm dead meat."

"You stole it from Richard Irons, I take it?"

"That's right, and what's more, he knows I took it. I didn't exactly steal it. I just got the design and sort of re-created it, but Irons wouldn't look at it that way."

"Is he really a hard man?"

"He's harder than tridium." There was a grim look on Edge's face. "I might as well level with you, Jerusha. This is going to be a dangerous trip. Irons knows that there is such a thing as tridium. He knows it's on a planet, but he doesn't know where. I talked too much, and it got back to him. Actually, I've been in hiding ever since. He's got his spies and agents out looking for me right now. If he catches me . . ."

He hesitated so long that Jerusha thought he was finished. "What will happen if he captures you, Captain?"

"I'd rather not go into that. He's capable of . . . anything. He has ways of making people do what he wants."

Jerusha sat there, thinking quickly. "All right. Tell me your terms."

"You'll go?"

"Not until I hear what you're offering. I expect to be paid, you know, and I'd like to do something with a little more future than just flying around in a spaceship."

Light touched Mark Edge's fine blue-gray eyes. He leaned forward and took her hand. "Jerusha," he said earnestly, "if we can get to Makon and get just a sample of tridium—and get back with it—every industrial giant on earth will give us anything we ask. Why, they'd be fighting to give us millions of dollars."

Sensing his earnestness, Jerusha made up her mind. "All right. I'm willing to go. I'll do the best job I can for you."

Edge squeezed her hand and then pounded the table. "That's great!" he said. And then an apprehensive look crossed his face. "But we can't go anywhere until we get more of a crew."

"How many do you have?"

"I've got Petroski. You've met him, and Zeno Thrax, and Tara Jaleel. I've got a crew chief. You haven't met him yet, a rough fellow called Studs Cagney. We have a small group of grunts—people to do the hard work. Not skilled, you understand, but we'll need them to do the mining when we get to Makon. And that's about it. We need more than that."

"Tell me what you need."

Jerusha listened as he outlined personnel needed before the *Daystar* could blast off. Then she sat silently, so silent that he said, "What's the matter?"

"I can get you some good people."

"You can!" Edge exclaimed. "That's wonderful!"

"They're very young . . ."

"If they can do their jobs, I don't care if they wear diapers!" Edge exclaimed. "Age is not a factor. Otherwise, I wouldn't have come looking for you. How soon can you get them together?"

"It won't take long. I might as well tell you—they're friends of mine, and we were the outcasts at the Academy. They've all been expelled for one reason or another, just as I was."

"I've been expelled a few times myself," Edge confessed. Then he said seriously, "Get them together as soon as you can, Jerusha. I've got to have a navigator, especially. A good one."

"None of them are navigators, but they're good at other things. I'll ask around."

"The sooner the better." Edge filled the two glasses with milk again. "All right, then. Here's to my new engineering assistant, Ensign Jerusha Ericson. Happy star flight, Jerusha."

"Happy star flight, Captain Edge."

The two drank the sweet, fresh, cool milk, and then Jerusha rose, saying, "I'll go back and start getting a crew together. Do you want to blindfold me?"

"No, you're a crew member of the *Daystar* now. I'll trust you just as you trust me."

Edge dropped her off at her room. "Here, you can reach me on this CommStat." He handed her a small, black square box with a recessed button and a built-in microphone. "Its stator is programmed to communicate directly to me," he said. "Don't try to contact me any other way."

"All right, Captain. And I'll do the best I can."

3
The Ensigns

Jerusha tried to make her small apartment more presentable. She was not by nature a housekeeper, and one of her problems at the Intergalactic Academy had proven to be demerits for not keeping her small room spotless. This was a strange trait, for Jerusha had an orderly mind and was an excellent engineer, but for some reason she found it very difficult to clean up after herself in her own quarters.

Glancing across the room at the clock she had attached to the wall with a piece of tape, she saw that her friends would be arriving at any moment. Quickly she stepped over to what served as a small kitchen and glanced at her supplies with a sense of gloom.

"Not much here in the way of refreshments," she muttered, noting the cakes that she had purchased with almost the last of her money. The smell of freshly brewed coffee, however, was in the air, and she counted to see if there were enough cups. "One . . . two . . . three . . . four . . . five . . . and one to spare." Then she said to Contessa, "Well, they're not coming here to be entertained anyhow."

Even as she spoke, a knock sounded at the door. She opened it and said, "Come in, Heck," to the boy who stood there.

Hector Jordan grinned broadly and stepped inside, stopping just long enough to give Jerusha a pinch, something he inevitably did.

Fifteen years old, Heck thought well of himself.

31

His name was Hector, but no one ever called him anything but Heck. He had bright red hair and blue eyes. He was overweight, which was understandable because he loved to eat. He also loved to wear fancy clothes and today was wearing a pair of light crimson trousers and a bright green shirt along with white boots. He looked, in effect, something like a rainbow. To make matters worse, he was partly color-blind and did not know, no matter how often he was told, that his clothes did not match.

"Got something to eat, Jerusha?" Heck picked up one of the cakes and bit off half of it. "These are good," he said and reached for more.

Jerusha leaped over and slapped his hand. "You wait until the rest come!"

"But I'm starved!" Heck said, looking longingly at the cakes and stuffing the other half into his mouth. "Can I have some coffee?"

"Sure. There's plenty of that anyway—for now."

Jerusha took a cup, poured it full of scalding black coffee, and watched him. Heck dumped in five heaping teaspoons of sugar, then added artificial powdered cream until his coffee looked little like the original substance. "You certainly know how to ruin a good cup of coffee," she said.

"To each his own, Jerusha." Heck grinned, licked his fingers, and looked longingly again at the cakes. "What's this meeting all about? I got your note, but you didn't explain anything."

"Let's wait until the others get here. I don't want to have to tell this story four times. What have you been doing?" she asked.

"Going hungry mostly." Heck did not seem to have lost any weight, though. His stomach was pudgy, his face was round, and he looked fully fed. "Ever since I got kicked out, I've been working nights washing dishes." He made a bitter face. "They used to call dishwashers in cafes 'pearl divers' back in the early days. Believe me, it's no fun."

He drifted over and tried to put his arm around Jerusha, who slapped his hand, and then he just grinned at her. It was impossible to hurt Heck Jordan's feelings. No matter how many times girls turned him down, he was never discouraged. "Come on. Give me a hint!" he said. "After all, I'm the electronic genius."

This sounded egotistical, but Jerusha knew that Heck was telling no less than the truth. He had put his first communicator together when he was only five years old and since then had mastered microelectronics as few grown men ever did. He was a cheerful young man, but Jerusha knew him to be selfish as well as vain. He was always sneaking around trying to find what would be best for *him.*

"Sit down, Heck. The others ought to be here very soon," Jerusha said. Almost automatically, she analyzed him. *He's wondering how much money is in this deal, and how he can get the best of it. He'll never change—he's always out for number one.* Aloud she said, "I hope Raina got my note. Have you seen her lately?"

"No. And to tell the truth, she gets on my nerves a little bit anyhow."

Jerusha smiled. "Girls that turn you down always get on your nerves."

"Turn me down? Why, she didn't turn me down. I just haven't decided yet to give her a break and take her out."

"Uh-uh!" Jerusha said. "Basically, you don't like Raina because she's a Christian, and she calls your hand when you do wrong."

"Do wrong? When did I ever do anything wrong?"

"All the time," Jerusha retorted, but she smiled. She really liked Heck, even though she knew he would take advantage of any situation. They sat and talked—Heck begging for cakes from time to time—until another knock sounded at the door.

"I'll get it," he said and went to the door. "Why, if it isn't Raina St. Clair. Come in, Raina. Haven't seen you in a long time." He kissed her noisily on the cheek.

"Oh, Heck!" Raina pushed him away.

Raina St. Clair was a small girl of fourteen. She had beautiful auburn hair with a widow's peak that made it very attractive. Her face was oval, and she had a dimple in her chin, which she claimed to hate. Her eyes were a strange shade of green. There was a frailness about her. She was not sickly, however, and although not athletic and having little stamina, still she was a healthy young woman.

"Come in, Raina. Don't pay any attention to Heck. You know *him.*"

Raina came over to give Jerusha a hug. "Yes, I know Heck," she said. "What's this meeting all about? You didn't say in your note."

"She's not telling anybody," Heck said grumpily. Then he crossed the room, plumped himself down in a chair, and reached for a cake.

He was thwarted when Jerusha snapped, "Leave those cakes alone!"

"You didn't bring us here to starve, did you?"

Ignoring him, Jerusha said, "I thought it'd be better to wait until Mei-Lani and Ringo get here. Then I can tell the whole story, and you can ask any questions you want."

This answer satisfied Raina, and the two girls sat down to talk. Heck broke in from time to time, then

34

snapped open his wrist computer and began working calculations.

After a few minutes a knock sounded at the door again, and when Jerusha answered it, she saw two young people standing in the hall. "Hello, Mei-Lani. Hello, Ringo."

The girl, Mei-Lani Lao, was clearly oriental. She was younger than the others, only thirteen. Her hair was black as jet, and her large brown eyes were almond shaped. She was even smaller than Raina, just one inch over five feet and weighing only ninety-five pounds. There was a reserved air about her, and she said shyly, "Hello, Jerusha. It's good to see you again."

"Good to see you, too, Mei-Lani."

Heck got up and tried to make himself charming. "Hello, Mei-Lani. You're looking beautiful today."

Mei-Lani gave him a cool glance and said, "Hello, Heck."

Jerusha knew Mei-Lani to be an unbelievably intelligent girl. Her favorite subjects had been history and the study of various languages. She read constantly and apparently never forgot anything. Heck had once said, "Her memory is like flypaper. Everything sticks to it, and she never loses it." She was wearing a simple gray dress without any ornament, but somehow the simplicity of it became her.

"Hi, Ringo," Heck said then, going over to greet the boy who had entered with Mei-Lani. "What's up, man?"

"Hello, Heck," Ringo said. He glanced around the room and greeted the others with a nod. There was a defensive air about Ringo Smith. At fourteen, he was neither particularly handsome nor overly tall. He had brown hair and strange-colored hazel eyes. He was wearing a pair of loose-fitting trousers and a brown pullover sweater. Underneath the sweater was a round medallion of some kind—Jerusha and the others knew he was never without it. He was a computer genius, having won awards for the creation of ten new programming protocols.

"Good to see you, Ringo," Jerusha said, coming over to shake his hand.

Her words warmed Ringo a little bit, and then his eyes went to Raina St. Clair. Jerusha already knew that Ringo Smith was completely infatuated with Raina, though he had never said anything. She also knew that he had had such a rough life being raised in a state orphanage that he had not learned to trust people. As the others greeted the newcomers, Jerusha was thinking, *Ringo wants love, but he doesn't know how to give it—or to receive it.* She felt sad as she sensed the boy's loneliness.

It was Heck, of course, who slapped his hands together and said, "Well, let's eat, and then you can tell us why you've called us all from our busy lives into this rat hole of an apartment."

"What a way you have with words, Heck," Jerusha said, making a face at him. Then she shrugged and said, "Well, I don't have much, but these cakes might be fairly good, and here's the coffee."

Raina helped her distribute the cakes, slapping Heck's hand when he tried to take two double portions. "Don't be such a pig, Heck!" she murmured.

"I'm not a pig! I'm just healthy! Why, I—"

Whatever Heck had intended to say was cut off by a very light knock at the door.

They all turned at once, and Raina asked in surprise, "Are you expecting someone else, Jerusha?"

"No . . . I'm not." For a moment Jerusha thought that it might be Captain Edge, at the same time knowing that whoever was on the other side of the door was not Edge. "I don't know who it could be."

"I—I think I might know," Mei-Lani said. When all eyes went to her, she flushed a delicate pink. "I asked a friend of mine to come."

"I'm not sure you should have done that, Mei-Lani," Jerusha said. "This is just between us."

The girl looked down for a moment. Then she lifted her beautiful brown eyes. She looked very vulnerable as she said, "He's a very good friend, and I wanted you all to meet him."

"Well, I guess we'll have to let him in," Jerusha said, not at all satisfied. Mei-Lani was so gentle that she could not find it in herself to do more than shrug her shoulders and give her a look of frustration. She crossed the room, opened the door, and stopped dead still, for standing there was one of the best-looking young men she had ever seen.

"Hello," he said.

He looked about sixteen and had the blackest hair and the blackest eyes Jerusha had ever seen. He was close to six feet and had a perfect build. Since he was wearing a light, tightfitting maroon shirt, the muscles of his chest and arms were clearly obvious. Jerusha knew at once that he was an athlete accustomed to working out.

"Well, come in," she said, "and let Mei-Lani introduce us. I suppose you're her friend."

Mei-Lani answered at once. "Yes, this is my friend, Dai Bando."

Quickly Mei-Lani called the names of the others, then said, "Dai's been very good to me since I was dropped from the Academy. As a matter of fact, I don't know what I would have done if it hadn't been for him."

No one ever asked about Mei-Lani's family, for she

never talked about them. They knew she was all alone in the world, and all had wondered how she would survive.

Jerusha said. "There are a few cakes left, Dai, if Heck here hasn't eaten them all."

"Thanks." The young man's words were brief, but he smiled, and two prominent dimples appeared, one in each cheek. He took a cake and nibbled on it, as Mei-Lani brought him coffee.

It was an awkward moment for Jerusha. She had to bring her plan before her friends, but she did not know this handsome boy that Mei-Lani had invited. She considered asking him to step outside, but that would hurt Mei-Lani. In addition to this, she liked what she saw in him. *He's very simple,* she thought, *but there's no harm in him. I don't know why Mei-Lani thought to ask him here, but I believe we can go on with the meeting.*

"Let's get on with it," Heck urged. "If you're not going to give us any more cakes, what's the plan?"

"All right. Everybody sit down, and I'll tell you. Last night I got home after being kicked out of the Academy like the rest of you, and there was a man here. He told me his name was Captain Mark Edge."

"Captain of what?" Ringo inquired, leaning forward. He was automatically suspicious of strangers, and the wariness on his face was obvious.

Jerusha tried to reassure him. "He's captain of a spaceship that he's built himself. It's called the *Daystar,* and he's looking for a crew."

"A crew?" Ringo said, brightening. "You mean there could be jobs in it?"

"I think there could be," Jerusha said, then added carefully, "but it's not the kind of jobs that you might be thinking of."

"What sort of a crew is it?" Mei-Lani asked.

Taking a deep breath, Jerusha said, "Well, here it is in a nutshell. Captain Edge has discovered a planet that has some very valuable minerals on it. If he can get there in the *Daystar*, get samples, and get back, he'll make a lot of money, and we'll all be well paid."

"It sounds good to me," Heck said airily. "What's hard about that?"

"Well, there are . . . problems."

"What sort of problems?" Ringo demanded. "Is what he's doing illegal?"

"No, not illegal but dangerous, I think." Jerusha saw the puzzlement on their faces, yet they all appeared interested. She cast her eyes toward Dai Bando, who had sat down on the floor with his back against the wall and was watching her attentively. She wondered what was going on in *his* mind. Then she continued explaining how Edge had once worked for a rich man and that the man might be dangerous.

"Who is it?" Heck demanded.

"Well, it's Sir Richard Irons."

"Wow!" Ringo said, awed. Irons was, perhaps, the richest man in the galaxy. He was certainly one of the most powerful. "You mean Irons is out to get this Captain Edge?"

"That's the way of it," Jerusha said. "So Captain Edge has this ship. It has a long fuselage section with delta-shaped wings on the aft and a long needlelike nose. I know it's not what we're used to, but it will make the journey. The only problem is that he hasn't been able to get enough crew."

"And he'll take us?" Raina asked. "Does he know we've all been expelled from the Academy?"

"Well, I haven't exactly told him that yet, though he knows about me," Jerusha admitted. "Still, he's

pretty desperate. And I might as well tell you now—
this *really* could be dangerous."

For some time the young people talked excitedly.
Ringo Smith was the most suspicious and asked question after question. Heck Jordan said, "Hey, it sounds
great. Cool! Let's do it!" Raina St. Clair was very
thoughtful. She said at one point, "I wouldn't go unless
I thought the Lord was leading me to do it." This
brought a rather disgusted look from Heck, who pro-
fessed to be tired of her Christianity. Mei-Lani said
nothing at all, but her eyes went frequently to Dai
Bando, and again Jerusha wondered what was between the two and why she had brought him.

Finally Ringo said, "This isn't getting us anywhere.
We've got to decide."

"Well, I'm ready to go," Heck said. "What about
you, Ringo? Have you got the nerve for it?"

Rather stung by the question, Ringo said, "Yes, I've
got the nerve for it!" He turned to Jerusha. "I'm willing
to try it, if everybody else is."

"So am I," Raina said. "I believe that it's something
we should do."

"What about you, Mei-Lani?" Jerusha said.

Mei-Lani hesitated, then said, "I can't go unless
Dai goes, too."

This came as a distinct shock to Jerusha. She
turned to Dai Bando and said, "What do you do, Dai?
All the rest of us have skills. Ringo's a computer man,
Heck is in electronics, Raina is a communications
expert, and Mei-Lani is a historian and a linguist, which
would be handy on any voyage."

"I don't do any of those things," Dai said rather
cheerfully.

"He's good at *physical* things." Mei-Lani spoke up
quickly. "He's very strong, and I've never seen anybody

40

with his balance and physical skills. Show them, Dai."

Dai Bando got to his feet and cocked his head to one side. He was very handsome, the girls were probably thinking, but Jerusha was also thinking, *Handsome isn't any use on a spaceship.*

"What do you want me to do, Mei-Lani?" Dai asked, smiling at her.

Mei-Lani said, "Do what you did for me last night."

Dai laughed. "Well, that's easy." He suddenly stooped over and balanced on his hands. Then he lifted one hand as he tilted his body. As they watched, he continued to stand on one hand, the other arm pressed flat against his side, his back arched.

"Did you ever see anyone who could do that?" Mei-Lani asked.

Dai looked at them from his upside-down position. Very slowly he lowered himself to the floor and did a perfect one-arm pushup, straightening up without any sign of effort. Then he flipped over and came to his feet in a catlike motion.

"Well, that's very impressive," Jerusha said, "but there aren't many calls for people to do acrobatics on a spaceship."

"Oh, he can do a lot more than that," Mei-Lani said. "Does anyone have a coin?"

"I've got one," Ringo said. He pulled a coin out of his pocket and handed it over to Mei-Lani, who gave it to Dai. "Show them, Dai."

Dai Bando held the coin between his thumb and forefinger, and then with no obvious effort at all he simply closed his fingers. The coin doubled up instantly.

"Wow!" Heck Jordan said. "I hope you don't do karate or any of that martial arts stuff."

"Oh, he does!" Mei-Lani said. "He's a black belt in all of them."

Jerusha was impressed by the physical skills of the boy, but she said, "I still don't know how all that could be used on a space voyage, except that we'll need some strong hands to do the mining." She considered for one moment, and as she did, she saw Mei-Lani watching her anxiously. Smiling at her, Jerusha said, "I've got the feeling you won't go if Dai doesn't. Is that right, Mei-Lani?"

Mei-Lani nodded and flushed again but said nothing.

"Well, Dai," Jerusha said, "if you want to come with us, you can ask Captain Edge if there's a place for you as a grunt. Grunts are the men that do the heavy work."

"Sounds fine to me."

For a while, the group talked excitedly about the new venture, and finally Jerusha said, "Well, I guess we're ready to go see the captain. Just one thing is missing. He doesn't have a navigator. And astronavigators aren't easy to find."

"I know one."

Everyone in the room turned to look at Dai Bando.

"You know an astronavigator?" Raina said.

"Yes, and a good one, too. She's my aunt."

4

The Navigator

The midafternoon sun was falling steadily, and the golden twilight began to appear quickly. Capt. Mark Edge stood at the spaceship window, staring at the spectacle. He was tired, for he had stayed up all the previous night working on the *Daystar.* He had had more than one tremendous argument with Ivan Petroski, and now he muttered, "Petroski has to be the hardest chief engineer to get along with in the whole galaxy!"

Wearily he turned back to the diagrams and papers that littered his desk, shuffled them until he found one, then plumped down in the hard plasto-steel chair and began to work with the drawings. His eyes burned, and with an exclamation of disgust he threw down the pen and rubbed them with the backs of his hands.

"Sometimes," he muttered almost desperately, "I don't think I'll ever get this ship off the ground."

Time passed slowly as Edge worked. Eventually he was interrupted by a tiny buzzing sound. Pulling the communicator from his belt, he pushed a button and growled, "What is it?"

The voice that came back sounded cheerful and clear. "Jerusha Ericson here, Captain Edge."

"So where are you? I've been waiting."

"We're just outside the gate. If you'll activate the door, I've got your crew for you."

"We'll see about that!" Edge muttered. The lack of

sleep made him terse. He walked through the hangar to the outer entrance, opened it, and then gaped at the young people who stood waiting. "It looks like a nursery of some kind!" he groused.

"I told you we were all young," Jerusha said calmly. She knew he was irritated, though. "If we can go inside, I'll introduce you to the crew and give you a breakdown on what they do."

"All right," Edge muttered. He ran his hand through his ruffled blond hair and walked away without another word.

As they entered the hangar, the young people stared at the ship.

"That's what we're supposed to fly around the galaxy in?" Ringo Smith snorted.

Heck Jordan, walking beside him, also seemed somewhat dismayed by the cruiser's rough exterior. But he said, "Well, if it'll get us up in the air, that's all I ask. All I want to be is rich and famous. I'm already good-looking," he confided.

Mei-Lani was walking with Dai Bando. She said nervously, "What do you think of all this, Dai?"

"I don't know," he admitted. "The ship looks all right to me. It might be fun to take a trip."

"You've never been on a spaceship, have you?"

"Nope! Never been very much of anywhere, really," Dai responded. He looked curiously at the *Daystar* and said, "So that's it."

"Doesn't look like much, does it?" Mei-Lani studied the lines of the vessel. "But with a good crew, she probably can do a lot."

"Wonder why people always refer to ships as she," Dai said.

"That's because back in the old days only men were on seagoing vessels. There were no women on board, so they more or less made the ships their wives. That's why they call them 'she.'"

Mei-Lani gave a little lecture on the nature of crews throughout history as they walked toward Edge's cabin. She did not often do this, but she had a vast knowledge of history and seemed to be able to call it up instantly.

When they were inside Edge's cabin, he said, "All right, Ensign Ericson. Introduce your people."

"This is Ringo Smith. He's the best man at computers you'll ever find. This is Hector Jordan, Heck for short. He's an electronics genius. This is Raina St. Clair, communications expert. And this is Mei-Lani Lao. She's a historian, a linguist, and knows everything about any people group we're liable to meet in outer space."

Edge seemed to be trying to implant their features on his brain. "I'll have to talk with each one of you individually," he said, "and check you out. And then you'll have to talk to the officers and pass their inspection." And then his eyes fell upon Mei-Lani's friend. "And who are you?"

"My name is Dai Bando."

"What kind of a name is that?"

"Oh, that's Welsh, Captain," Mei-Lani said quickly. "The Welsh occupied what was a part of the old world called Wales. They're famous for their music and are a very spiritual people."

"Spiritual, are you? You're a preacher, then?"

"Nope!" Dai said cheerfully. "Not me. I wouldn't know how to preach a sermon."

"What do you do?"

"He's very strong, Captain," Mei-Lani said. "And he has very good reflexes."

"Well, we do need some strong backs," Edge admitted.

Captain Edge was not happy with the group of teenagers. It had seemed a good idea at the time, since he could not recruit adults, but now, looking them over, he was feeling some reservations.

His eyes remained fixed on Dai Bando. The others would be checked out by experts, but this boy who was almost as tall as he was especially interested him. He was obviously strong, and they would need that sort of man to do the mining on Makon. Still, Edge was in a bad humor and felt the need to impress upon the crew that he was the captain. "What's this about reflexes?" he asked.

Dai shrugged. "I've always had good reflexes."

"Well, give me a sample."

Dai winked at Mei-Lani and said, "Can I borrow that handkerchief?"

Mei-Lani was wearing a bright scarlet silk neckerchief, and she took it off and handed it to him. Dai Bando formed it into a blindfold and stepped up to Edge. He tied the scarf over his own eyes and said, "This is just a little game I play sometimes. Hit me."

"What did you say?" Edge demanded.

"See if you can hit me in the face."

Edge glanced around and saw that the others were watching carefully. "You don't want me to do that, son. I might hurt you."

"Take your best shot," Dai said. "I don't think you'll hurt me."

He was stung by the boy's assurance, and Edge's hand flashed out. He did not use his fist, intending just to slap the young man, but as fast as he moved, he barely touched the boy's face. As soon as his hand made contact, Dai jerked his head back, and there was no damaging contact at all.

Somewhat shocked, Edge said grudgingly, "That's pretty good."

"Well, as I said, I've always had pretty good reflexes. Try again."

This time Edge tried to trick him. He shot out his left hand, and Dai pulled his face away quicker than thought. But Edge had aimed another blow with his right hand. He was certain this would catch Dai Bando as he moved away, but again his hand barely touched the side of the boy's face. Edge's face reddened, for a giggle went up from some of the girls. He tried harder. But no matter how hard he tried, he was unable to make contact.

This boy's reflexes are superhuman, he thought. Aloud he said, "Well, OK. You passed that test." He watched as Dai Bando took off the scarlet neckerchief and handed it back to Mei-Lani. "That's pretty good. You'd be a hard one to beat in any kind of a fight."

"I never lose," Dai Bando remarked. It would have sounded egotistical from anyone else, but somehow Edge got the idea that Dai Bando had little ego. He was merely stating a fact.

"I can sign you on as a grunt, but you'll have to satisfy the crew chief, and he's a tough one."

"That's fine, Captain." Dai Bando nodded. "I'll be glad to make the trip."

"All right. Now, how much has Ensign Ericson told all of you about this plan of mine?"

"It sounds like a real picnic, Cap," Heck replied airily.

"It's Captain, not *Cap!*" Edge snapped. "And it's not going to be a picnic! If you've got that idea in your mind, you might as well leave now!"

"Oh, you just have to understand Heck, Captain," Raina said quickly. "That's just his way."

"Well, his way will have to change. Now, I want to know more about your experience."

Edge listened as the four young people recounted their backgrounds and their specialties. When they were through, he said, "So you were all chunked out of the Intergalactic Academy, is that right?"

"I would have left anyway," Heck said. "They're too stuffy in that place. This looks like my kind of life, *Captain.*" He stressed the word and grinned brazenly at Edge.

Edge studied the boy, then his eyes went to Jerusha. "Are you answering for all these people, Ensign?"

"I'll answer for their abilities," Jerusha said coolly. "And I think they can stand in good comparison with the rest of your crew."

For a long moment Edge hesitated, then he slapped his hand against his side in a gesture of finality. "All right," he said firmly. "You'll have to talk to the other officers—the people you will be working with—but I feel that as soon as we get a navigator, we'll be ready." He passed his hand over his forehead in a gesture of despair. "I've tried everywhere, and I can't find anyone. I can't just put an ad on the local television, you know, asking for a navigator. Richard Irons would be down on me like a hawk."

"Captain?"

Edge looked up at Dai Bando, who was gazing at him peculiarly. "I think I can solve your problem."

"Don't tell me you can navigate."

"Oh, no, sir. Not me. I'm not technical. But a relative of mine is a great navigator."

This statement caught the captain's attention. "Well, where is he? What's his experience?"

48

"I thought you might be interested, so I brought my relative along."

"Well, go bring him in."

"Yes, sir."

Dai Bando left the cabin, and as the door closed Edge looked at Jerusha. "Did you know about this, Ensign?"

"Yes, I did."

"But, you didn't say anything."

"I wasn't sure that the candidate would suit you. You'll have to make up your own mind."

Something about Jerusha's reply gave Edge an uneasy feeling. However, he said, "All right, but if he can find his way to the men's room, I'll have to take him. I've got to have a navigator."

He wondered at the smiles that crossed the faces of some of the young people, thinking, *What's that all about?* While he waited, he talked further to them about their experience.

He was about to tell them more of the plan, when the door opened and Dai Bando walked in, followed by a woman. She was about fifty. She had silver hair. She was small. She had intensely dark blue eyes.

"This is my aunt, Bronwen Llewellen," Dai announced.

"How do you do, Captain?" the woman said, fixing the officer with a steady glance. "I understand you must have a navigator."

Edge felt trapped and betrayed. He looked accusingly at Jerusha, who appeared to sense his irritation.

"I'm sorry, ma'am," he said to the woman, "but this is going to be a rough voyage. It's no job for an—" He was going to say "an older woman" but bit the words off and changed them to "amateur."

"Well, I have had some experience, Captain, and I'm not quite as old as you may be thinking."

The woman's instant grasp of what he had intended to say startled Captain Edge. He cleared his throat, then ran his hand nervously through his hair, something he often did when he was upset. "I don't want to upset you, Mrs. Llewellen, but truly this is going to be a very difficult trip—and dangerous. I couldn't be responsible for taking a lady of . . . your age . . . on such a journey."

Silence fell over the room, and Edge felt himself growing increasingly uncomfortable. The woman was studying him. He saw the serenity about her—and something else that he could not define. He'd noticed that Jerusha seemed exceptionally perceptive, and he turned to her. "What do you think, Ensign?"

"I think you'd better consider her, Captain," she said. "I don't know anything about her navigational abilities, but I do believe that she's qualified for a long space flight, perhaps—" she glanced at Heck "—more than some of the rest of us are."

Suddenly Mei-Lani said, "Captain, you don't know much history, do you?"

Rather insulted, Edge said, "What do you mean by that, young lady?"

"Why, this is *Bronwen Llewellen*. Even you must have read about her."

A hasty harsh reply leaped to the captain's lips, but then a memory nudged him. "Bronwen Llewellen," he murmured and looked at the woman with interest. "I do know that name . . ."

"You should, Captain," Mei-Lani said quietly. "She was the navigator on the *Orion* when it made the most difficult space voyage in history. She took the *Orion* to the very edge of the known universe and brought it back safely." Mei-Lani smiled at the captain's face, seeing how astonished he was. "If she chose to wear it, she could wear the Legion of Merit, the highest order given by the Intergalactic Federation."

Now Edge remembered the story. So this small woman had been navigator on that voyage. He had simply not associated this silver-haired fifty-year-old with the vibrant young woman who had guided the *Orion*.

"My apologies, Mrs. Llewellen," he said abjectly. "I don't know what I was thinking about."

"That's quite all right, Captain."

Edge shifted nervously, then said, "But I still can't take you on this trip, you know. It's just too dangerous."

Then it was that Capt. Mark Edge got his first evidence of the spiritually attuned sort of woman Bronwen Llewellen was. She stood with the marks of aging in her face and said quietly, "God has assured me I will die on Earth, Captain. The rest of you may die in space, or on Makon, but not me."

"*God* has told you that?" Edge was shocked by her words. "God has actually told you that?"

"Why, yes, He has. Though not in audible words. Doesn't God tell you things, Captain?"

Mark Edge was speechless. His eyes ran around the group, and he saw smiles on the faces of Dai Bando and Jerusha Ericson and Raina St. Clair. "No, ma'am," Edge said, "God has never said anything to me."

"Oh, I'm sure He has," Bronwen Llewellen said quietly. And then a smile turned up the corners of her lips. "I think you just haven't been listening to Him."

5

Six Babies, a Mutt, and a Grandma

W ill you please keep this blasted dog away from me!"

Jerusha was walking beside Edge as the pair led the new crew members from the captain's office. Contessa, who had not gotten more than a foot away from the captain all the time, now pressed against his leg, almost upsetting his balance. She looked up at him with adoring eyes and growled happily in her throat, nipping at his hand.

"She loves you, Captain. You ought to be flattered." Jerusha smiled. It amused her that the huge dog had taken such a liking to the captain, for Mark Edge obviously did not like animals in general and big dogs especially.

"Next thing I know she'll be sitting in my lap or trying to sleep in my bed," Edge complained. He shot a glance at Jerusha and saw that she was laughing at him. "It's not funny!" he said.

"No, sir. Of course not."

He led them to a large workroom off to the right of the main hangar, where they were greeted by a short muscular man with thinning black hair and bloodshot dark eyes.

There was a rough and brutal look about the man that Jerusha distrusted immediately. The impressions she got from him were cloudy but definitely not good.

This one will have to be watched, she thought, *but I suppose the captain has to take whoever he can get.*

"This is Studs Cagney, our crew chief," Edge announced. He swept his hand around the small group that had accompanied him, saying, "Chief, these are the new members of our crew."

Cagney stared from one to another of the new additions, and then snorted. "Six babies, a mutt, and a grandma!"

Edge shrugged impatiently. "We have to take what is available, chief. I've got one volunteer for your crew."

"Which one of the babies is it?"

"This one. His name is Dai Bando."

"What kind of a nutty name is that?"

"It doesn't matter what kind of a name it is. The fact is, he's strong enough to do the work we'll run into on Makon."

Cagney stared at Dai's smooth, unruffled face, shook his head, then sneered. "I won't have a baby like him in my crew! I'm not set up to run a nursery!"

Mei-Lani spoke up suddenly. "I think you'll find him tough enough, sir. Why don't you give him a try?"

Shooting a glance of disdain at the diminutive oriental girl, Cagney sneered again. "I don't want to hurt him."

Keeping a straight face, Edge said, "I think he's a little tougher than you might believe, chief. Just grab him and throw him out of here. If you can put him on his back, I won't insist on his going."

A light of anticipation came into the burly man's eyes. "OK, I'll do that. Come here, sonny. If you want to lie down now, I won't hurt you."

Dai said nothing but kept his eyes fixed on the muscular chief, who was advancing toward him with both hands extended.

Studs Cagney was obviously the veteran of many brawls. He had scars on his face, and despite the fact that he was so big, he moved lightly. Now he came at Dai with his left hand out, intending to grab him, but before Cagney could move further, he found his wrist grasped in what must have felt like a band of iron. Grunting, he tried to jerk it back and found it held fast, as if it had been set in cement.

With a cry of rage, Cagney threw his other fist straight at the boy's face. The blow went harmlessly over Dai's shoulder. Cagney was suddenly lifted in the air and spun around. And then he was stretched flat on the floor, helpless until the grip on his wrist was released.

Studs Cagney was plainly a violent man and not one who thought deeply. Without his making a sound other than a grunt of rage, a knife appeared in his hand, and he lunged at Dai Bando.

"Don't do it, Studs!" the captain shouted.

Cagney was beyond listening. He drove the knife directly at the young man's chest.

But instead of its hitting flesh and bone, the boy turned his body sideways, and the knife went by him. He reached out, again grabbed the thick wrist of the crew chief, twisted it, and the knife fell with a clatter to the floor.

Once again, Cagney uttered a cry of rage, but he could not shake his fist free.

Bando reached down quickly, picked up the knife, and held it pointed at Cagney's throat. "I believe you dropped this," he said pleasantly, a slight smile on his lips.

"And I think you lost this argument, chief," Edge said. Studs Cagney ruled his crew by the power of his burly arms and the blows of his fists, but this boy had handled him as if he were a child. "I also think you've got a new member on your crew."

Cagney glared at the captain but had no reply. Then he turned baleful eyes on Dai Bando. "You'll do in a fight, I guess, but it takes more than that to be a member of *my* crew. Come along."

As the two walked away, Mei-Lani said, "He's a violent man."

"Very violent," Jerusha agreed. "Do you *have* to have men like that to run the ship?"

Edge looked at her. Then he said, "Raina, I want you to meet Zeno Thrax. He's our communications officer. You'll be his assistant. Jerusha, you can take the others around to talk to the rest of the crew. They should all be at their work stations."

"Very well, Captain."

Raina and the captain found Thrax inside the ship, seated before a fantastically complicated keyboard. He rose at once when the two came in and nodded when he received the captain's orders to check out the girl's ability.

After Edge left, Thrax said, "I'm happy to have you aboard, you and your friends."

"Well, thank you, Lieutenant Thrax." Raina had never seen an albino before and found the communications officer very interesting. Being a straightforward girl, she asked, "Which planet are you from?"

"I'm from Mentor Seven."

"I suppose Mei-Lani would know about that one, but I don't. What's your planet like? Is it beautiful?"

"No, it's very ugly."

"Ugly? Are you serious?"

"You would think so. There are very few trees. It looks like a desert. Very hot on one side and freezing on the other side. All of my people live underground."

"I don't think I would like *that*," Raina said. "Why are you going on this rather dangerous journey, Miss St. Clair?"

"Oh, just call me Raina. I suppose I'll be Cadet or Ensign or something, but Raina is fine."

"That's a very beautiful name, Raina St. Clair," the albino said. He studied her.

Raina thought there was an air of loneliness about him, yet his eyes were rather playful at the same time. He had a wry sense of humor, she soon discovered. Soon they were deep in a discussion of communications systems.

He pointed to the encryption encoder to the right of the communication console. "Raina, could you please adjust the encryption format from J74y to Beta 23a76."

Raina reached around Thrax and flipped an assortment of control switches until the encoder displayed Beta 23a76. "Lieutenant Thrax, can I make a suggestion?" she asked politely.

"Certainly."

"The Beta codes were broken about three months ago. I would suggest adjusting the encryption code to a newer format."

"What do you suggest?" he asked knowingly.

"The ZP code with a slight variation . . . say, ZP432c15?"

The albino smiled approvingly as he adjusted the encoder to her suggestion.

Raina found herself liking the ghostly white lieutenant. She asked, "Might you be a Christian, Lieutenant Thrax?"

"A Christian? No, I don't think so." He looked at her for a moment, then said, "What is a Christian? Does it have something to do with communication security clearances?"

"No, it has to do with religion."

"Oh, we have our own religion on Mentor Seven—our priests. I never took much part in it," Thrax admitted. He regarded her for a moment more. "Perhaps you will tell me more about your religion when we have spare time. I would like that very much."

"I'd be glad to, Lieutenant," she said and smiled at him winsomely.

Tara Jaleel eyed Ringo with disdain. "You're not very large," she said. "Can you fight?"

"Fight?" Ringo stared back. "I'm not a soldier. I'm a computer operator."

"I have little respect for anyone who cannot fight." She reached out suddenly and took his arm. Her grasp was steely, and she squeezed until Ringo had to bite his lip to keep from crying out.

"Bah! You're soft and flabby!" Jaleel said with disgust. "You will not last long, I think."

"There's more to life than fighting!" Ringo exclaimed. "Physical strength isn't everything!"

His words did not seem to go down well with the tall black woman. She wagged her head in disgust. "There's something wrong about a male who doesn't like to fight."

"I think there's something wrong with a woman who *does* like to fight!"

"You think that, do you? Then you're wrong! My people have always been fierce fighters, the women as well as the men. Before this trip is over, I will insist that you improve yourself. I will set up a regular series of exercises, and you will learn some of the arts of battle." Ringo did not like this woman because she embarrassed him. He knew that he was not strong physically. As a matter of fact, he felt inferior in most situations. However, there was a look in Tara Jaleel's eyes that convinced him this was no time to argue. "All right," he said. "If the captain orders it, I'll do it."

Ivan Petroski waited until Jaleel was finished talking with Ringo Smith. When she left, he approached Ringo.

"She's a rough one, isn't she?" He had to look up to speak to the ensign. "All she thinks about is killing somebody or fighting somebody. She's the right person for weapons officer."

"She wants me to learn to do that martial arts stuff. I don't think I can do it. Dai Bando is good at that, but that doesn't help you with a computer!"

"I suspect you'll have to go through the motions anyway." The dwarf was studying the boy. "I don't think it's normal taking such young people into deep space."

"We've all been through part of the program at the Space Academy."

"Well, the Academy's one thing, but it's another thing to keep a spaceship running. This ship runs mostly on computers. Tell me what you know about computers."

Ringo thought for a moment before responding. "If this ship is configured like most of the rest I know about, there's a central mainframe computer that's linked to several smaller subsystem computers throughout the ship, such as navigations, engineering, communications, and medical. The mainframe also monitors the ship's structural integrity, shields, and life support. Command access to the subsystems is controlled by the mainframe—"

Petroski interrupted. "All right, all right. I can see you know your way around. Come along, and I'll show you the main computer, and we'll give you a few drills."

Edge was back in his cabin and had just served Jerusha a drink. This time it was not milk but some unpleasant-tasting concoction that was advertised and sold as being a delicious beverage. Edge made a face. "This stuff is awful!" he complained.

Contessa, who was right beside him, reared up and put her paws on his extended legs. She licked his face before he could move.

"Get this animal off of me!" he yelped.

"Don't you like her even a little bit?" Jerusha asked.

"No! I don't like dogs! And anyway, this is too much dog." He stood, looked down at her, and said, "I hope you don't think we're going to take her with us."

"She goes where I go."

"Absolutely not!"

"If Contessa doesn't go, I don't go! And I suspect some of the rest won't go either."

"That's blackmail!"

"You'll like Contessa after a while. She's very useful."

"Useful for what, besides making a pest out of herself?"

Sitting on the table in front of Jerusha was a bottle of the soft drink. The top was firmly attached. It was made of crimped metal and required a special opener to get it off. "Useful for this . . ." She picked up the bottle and held it in front of the dog. "Open it, Contessa."

Contessa reached out, put her lower teeth under the bottle, and with ease flipped the top off. "See? She *is* useful." Jerusha was smiling at the captain, but she had to know that he was not amused. She sipped her beverage and agreed, "This is pretty bad stuff."

Captain Edge sat once again, put down his drink, and folded his arms. He tried to ignore Contessa, who was crowding ever closer. "I'm worried about this trip," he said at last. He looked over at her and said, "You sense that, don't you?"

"I know you're troubled."

"It's going to be a hard trip." He stirred uneasily and gave her a wary glance. "Why are you looking at me like that?"

"Because you're not telling me everything. You're keeping something back. What is it?"

"I've told you all about Richard Irons. He'll have us for lunch if he catches us. You too. All the crew."

Jerusha studied him, then shook her head. "No, you're not hiding that."

"How do you know I'm hiding anything?" he demanded.

"I just sense you're hiding something from me. Captain, you'd better tell me now. We're going with you, but it's better to know the truth."

A short laugh escaped Edge. He ran his hands through his hair in a gesture of despair. "You and Thrax! Sometimes I'm convinced he can read my mind! And I've got a suspicion that our new navigator—she's peculiar, too!" He stared at her defiantly. "Anyway, I guess I might as well tell you the truth. Makon is inhabited by a not very bright race of people called the Dulkins. I met them when I was there on my exploration."

"You got the tridium from them, didn't you? There was no other way for you to get it."

"Yes, I did. That was the way of it." The captain looked at her guiltily.

"They didn't give it to you voluntarily, did they?"

"Well, they showed it to me, but when I offered to buy it they said no, so I had to—well, I had to *borrow* it."

"In other words, you stole it."

"I don't like to put it like that."

"There's no other way to put it," Jerusha said calmly. "And now we're going back to Makon, and you have to face the people you stole from."

"Look, they're ignorant, dirty, no imagination at all. All they know how to do is to grub in the earth. I don't intend to *rob* them," he said defensively.

"I'm afraid that's exactly what you do intend, Captain Edge, but I must tell you that none of us will help you do that. I don't know about the rest of your crew, but we're not thieves or pirates."

"You're putting this all wrong," Edge protested.

"I don't think I am," Jerusha said.

She was very attractive. Her ash-blonde hair fell down over her smoothly fitting tunic. Her eyes were very dark blue, and her complexion was flawless. But for all her beauty, the captain perceived she had a hard edge.

"It's not very wise for you to sit in the captain's cabin and tell him he's a crook."

"You're no better than Sir Richard Irons, Captain."

Edge glowered at her. He tried to think of something to say, but no matter how his mind searched for an answer, he could find none. He knew that the girl was telling the exact truth, and somehow this disturbed him greatly. Angrily he rose and said, "I have work to do, and I would suppose you do too. You'll come to understand the ways of the world a little bit better."

"Or *you'll* come to understand the ways of God a little bit better," Jerusha said as she left the cabin.

Jerusha went about her duties, wondering what the Dulkins were like—and what she would do if Captain Edge insisted on acting like a pirate.

6

The Shadow

The engines of the *Daystar* began to glow as Captain Edge went through the checklist he and Ivan had put together. The bottom thrusters began to gently lift the craft from the ground, producing a windstorm inside the docking port. Edge spoke into his communicator, ordering the ceiling doors of the port to open. Slowly the two giant doors slid apart, revealing open sky above them.

"Edge to Petroski."

"She looks good, Captain. All my boards show green lights."

Daystar's thrusters became louder as Edge fed more power to them. The awkward-looking ship rose higher and higher until it cleared the roof of the docking port.

"This is always the scariest part for me," Jerusha informed Ivan as they monitored the engineering computer display. "I was in a training ship at the Academy last quarter. Two of the thrusters blew, and we dropped like a rock forty feet to the ground."

Petroski didn't crack a smile. She suspected he was nervous himself.

"There's the signal," he said. "Now let's ease the engines into one-eighth power."

The ground raced by as *Daystar*'s Mark V engines thrust the ship overland faster and faster. Within a few seconds *Daystar* was traveling at close to the speed of sound. Captain Edge adjusted the ailerons on the forward stabilizers, and the spacecraft's nose pointed skyward. Within seconds more, *Daystar* had accelerated through the stratosphere, thermosphere, exosphere, and finally through the final remnants of the ionosphere.

The heavens looked black, and stars spangled the darkness, making points of light. Once they left the earth's atmosphere, the stars became much brighter.

"Well, we're off," Mei-Lani said, standing at the porthole, watching the sky. She turned to Raina, and the girls smiled at each other.

"Are you glad we came?" Raina asked.

"Oh, yes," Mei-Lani said. Her dark eyes glowed, and again she glanced out the window. "This reminds me of a poem I read once. . . ." Mei-Lani frowned. "I can't remember waht it was!"

Raina laughed and put her arm around the smaller girl. "That's the first time you ever failed to remember *anything* that I know of. But it's a beautiful line, and that's what we've done."

"Hey, what's coming down?"

The girls looked up to see Heck Jordan. He was wearing a vivid purple tunic and a pair of mismatched lavender trousers today. He squeezed between them and stared out the porthole. "Quite a sight, isn't it?" He attempted to put his arms around both girls, and each of them slapped his hands. "Hey, just trying to be friendly!" He grinned and said, "Let's go get some chow."

"We just had a meal," Mei-Lani protested.

"That's right," Raina said, "and after all that food you put down, you couldn't possibly be hungry."

"I'm like a camel." Heck grinned, pulling a candy bar from his pocket. "I eat all I can, every chance I get. You never know when you might have a long hungry stretch coming on." He began to munch on the candy but was interrupted when Ivan Petroski suddenly popped in and shouted, "Jordan, stop stuffing yourself and come to the bridge!"

"Right, Chief," Heck said cheerfully. He winked at the girls. "They couldn't run this bucket of bolts without me. See you later."

Heck followed Petroski down the narrow corridor that ran through the center of the ship. When they reached the bridge, Petroski let out an angry yelp. "Hey, you mangy dog! Get away from there!"

Heck peered over Petroski's head to see that Contessa had reared up on the control panel and was devouring the last of what apparently had been Ivan's lunch. She swallowed, dropped to all fours, then wagged her tail and barked happily.

Petroski tried to shove her out of the way, but she was too big and heavy for him. "I ought to shoot you with a Neuromag on full force!" he exclaimed. He finally succeeded in moving the huge animal aside, and as she trotted off, he muttered, "It's bad luck to have a dog aboard. I wish we hadn't brought her!"

"Oh, she's OK, Petroski."

"Call me Lieutenant!" Petroski exclaimed angrily.

Edge had determined to maintain a military setup with his officers, much as at the Space Academy, even though they were not military, and Petroski was very jealous of his title. He stepped to the control panel, his eyes running over the gauges. "Pay attention, Ensign Jordan. We're having some trouble with the inertia systems." He wagged his head woefully. "It's too bad we lost our last electronics man."

"He died, you mean?"

"No, he got a cushy job with the Inter-Stellar Transport System."

"Well, you've got me. I'm better than he was."
Heck grinned confidently. "What's the trouble?" He listened as the engineer outlined the problem and at once said, "I'll get my tools and probe this baby. We'll have it running like a fine watch."

Back in the observatory, Raina was still watching the stars. Mei-Lani had gone to her station, and, standing alone at the porthole, Raina enjoyed the throbbing sensation as the ship pulsed through space. There was little sense of speed, and the deck of the *Daystar* was as steady as a room back on Earth.

Hearing a bark, she turned and saw Contessa come bounding in. As the huge dog trotted up to her, she put out her hand and laughed, then petted the animal's broad forehead. "Hello, Contessa. What are you doing here?"

Then Jerusha appeared and frowned at the sight of her dog. "I told you to behave, Contessa!"

"Oh, she's all right. I like dogs," Raina said. She saw that Jerusha had a ball in her hand. "Is that Contessa's ball?"

"Oh, yes. She has so little chance for exercise on a ship that I like to let her chase it for a while. It gets tiresome though. She likes to get the ball, but she won't give it back to me."

"Let me see it." Raina caught the ball deftly, then held it up. "Here, Contessa," she said, her eyes alight with fun. She tossed the ball down the corridor, and Contessa whirled and scrambled after it, her claws scratching on the deck. Finally she caught up with the rolling ball, grabbed it, and plopped down, eyeing Raina but making no effort to return the ball.

Jerusha looked out of the window, seemingly taken by the spectacular spangled heavens.

"Your parents were very devout Christians, weren't they, Raina?" she asked suddenly.

"Yes, they were missionaries—to the planet Zocor."

"Is that where you grew up?"

"Yes, and it was a very hard place. People there are savage. More than once I thought we were going to be killed by them, but God always brought us through."

Jerusha turned to look at her. She asked quietly, "Were you afraid?"

Raina considered the question, then said, "I don't think I was, really. My mother and father taught me so well that if we lived, we were with God—and if we died, we were even closer to God. Not that I was anxious to die, but they always taught me that heaven was my real home and any other place is just a little trip I'm on. Did you ever think of it like that, Jerusha?"

Jerusha looked embarrassed. "I guess I'm not as religious as I should be."

"Has Christ ever come into your life?" Raina asked.

"Yes, He has—but I know I could be a better Christian," she said. Then she changed the subject. "I guess I'd better get to the captain's station. He wants me to learn how to con the ship."

"You may be a captain yourself one day," Raina said. "You're smart enough, Jerusha."

Raina had great admiration for Jerusha. She watched the girl and Contessa leave the room, then murmured to herself, "She's so strong, but someday she's going to meet something she can't handle. Then she's going to see her need for trusting Jesus Christ day by day."

The original crew of the *Daystar* at first found it difficult to accept the newcomers, but they soon discovered that all of them were excellent at their jobs. Zeno Thrax, especially, was complimentary. Speaking to the captain on the second watch—the two were alone at the helm—he said, "You did a good job of recruiting, Captain."

"You like the Junior Space Rangers, do you, Zeno?"

"They're very good at their jobs."

"They're very young," Captain Edge said. "That means they have some liabilities."

"You mean that older people don't bring liabilities?" Thrax smiled.

Edge laughed. "No, I guess that's right. Some of the oldest crew members I've had were the most immature in a way. What do you make of Ensign Ericson?"

"Now there's some maturity for you." Thrax's pale face glowed as though an inner light filled him. He thought for a moment, then said, "She's highly sensitive to what is going on in people's thinking. She's almost a mind reader. Isn't, of course."

"That's a good thing! One of you is enough on this ship." Edge looked over at Zeno. "Must be nice to be supersensitive to what others are thinking—about themselves and about you."

"Not really."

Surprised at the albino's instant response, Edge asked, "Why not? Then you would always know just where you stood with people."

"You'd think so, but it doesn't work like that. You see, Captain, people often deceive themselves. What they think of themselves isn't what they are. For example, you think you're a very tough fellow, but deep down you have some soft spots."

"Oh, come on, Zeno. There's nothing soft about me."

"You see? You really think you're a hard-nosed captain who has no time for anything that's not business." Thrax smiled. "But there's another side to you that, for some reason, you hate to admit having. You think it's—as the old Earthlings would say—sissified."

Captain Edge opened his mouth to argue, but he saw the light of humor dancing in the eyes of the Mentorian. Somehow Edge was embarrassed, and he muttered, "Well, it's a great relief to see that you're not perfect at reading minds. What about the rest of the new crew?"

As always, Mark Edge was glad to get the views of his first officer, for he trusted the judgment of the pale-skinned man. Finally he asked, "And what do you make of our navigator?"

"Very beautiful lady, indeed. Not just outside. She's attractive enough, but inside she has a beautiful spirit."

"I just hope she can navigate this crate."

"She'll do that, sir."

At that moment Bronwen Llewellen herself walked onto the bridge. She was wearing a simple gray dress and looked rather regal. "Here's the change in course, Captain Edge."

"Thank you, Mrs. Llewellen." He looked at the paper she handed him and frowned. "Are you sure this is right? It seems to be taking us off course."

A smile touched the woman's face, and she nodded. "I think you'll find that's correct. There are some meteor fields ahead that we need to avoid. I'll keep a close watch on the course, however." She was silent for a moment, then said, "Please be careful, Captain."

Surprised, Edge looked at her. "Be careful about what, Mrs. Llewellen?"

"Oh, you can call me Bronwen. I'm not an officer. Just a lowly navigator."

"Well, then, Bronwen, be careful about what?"

The features of Bronwen assumed a solemn aspect. "I don't know," she confessed finally. "I just think something's—not right."

With that word, she walked away, and Edge turned to his first officer. "What do you make of that, First?"

"I think you'd better pay attention. She seems to be one of those people with a sense of things that most of us lack."

"You mean she's a fortune-teller?"

Thrax shook his head. "I don't mean anything, Captain. I just feel that you'd better pay attention."

Two days later, the captain was surprised when Jerusha came unexpectedly to his cabin. He saw the light go on that signaled someone was outside, and when he said, "Come in," the door opened. He laid down his book and said, "What is it, Ensign?"

"Sir, I think something is wrong."

"You, too? Bronwen's been telling me for a couple of days now that something's wrong. But she can't put a finger on anything. I'm not superstitious, you know . . ."

"This isn't superstition. I found something on the tracking screen that I can't explain. You'd better come with me, sir. I think it's serious."

"Explain."

"As you know, Ivan and Heck have been working on a few bugs that developed with the inertia system, so our scanners have been on- and off-line several times. When I started 'A' shift today, the scanners had been off for a couple of hours. Ivan put them back on-line, and the scanner picked up an echo just on the edge of scanning range. Thinking it was just another glitch in the system, I didn't pay too much attention to it . . ."

The captain rolled his eyes. "Let's go look at the display."

She led him to the bridge and pointed down at the screen before her. "Do you see that?"

Captain Edge leaned forward and narrowed his eyes. "I don't see anything."

"It's very faint. It comes, and it goes. Mostly it goes," Jerusha said.

"Jerusha, it's probably just some sort of a glitch in the computer, as you thought. Have Jordan look at it."

"I have had him look at it, sir, and he says the computer's working perfectly. I don't think you can ignore this. If it were just a glitch, it wouldn't be moving across the display. It comes nearer, then fades back. It's done this several times now."

Edge turned and looked at her. He studied the ash-blonde hair and the intense dark blue eyes. Her face was too strong for beauty-queen attractiveness, but— no question about it—she was attractive. "What do *you* think it is, Jerusha?"

"I think it's a shadow. Someone's tailing us!"

Instantly Mark Edge grew cautious. "That's bad news," he murmured. He stared back at the screen. "We'll have to shake them off, if it is someone shadowing us."

The next day Captain Edge stayed at the bridge almost constantly. He tried everything he knew to escape whatever was following them. *It's as if they know every maneuver I'm going to make before I make it!* he thought.

Once Bronwen Llewellen came onto the bridge and stood beside him, watching the screen silently.

Feeling her presence, the captain said, "I've tried everything I can think of to get away from that dot."

"What do you think it is, Captain?"

"I'm afraid it's one of Sir Richard Irons's men. Maybe Irons himself. He'd love to catch me and make me tell—" He broke off, not wanting to share everything with this woman who seemed to know a great deal already. "Well," he said hurriedly, "I'll have to try something else to escape."

Bronwen Llewellen looked up at the man and seemed interested in the strong planes of his face. She held his gaze for a long time, then said, "There're some things that a person can't escape, Captain Edge." With this enigmatic statement she left the bridge, leaving him puzzled and a little troubled.

"Well, I'll escape *this* thing!" He thumped the screen with his forefinger and threw his energies back into directing the *Daystar.*

7

A Traitor Unmasked

W e may have to turn back."
  Captain Edge's face was grim with fatigue and strain. His lips were almost white, and his eyes were narrowed as he stared at the screen before him. He swung around to face Petroski and Jerusha Ericson. "We may have to turn back," he repeated.

"We can't do that, Captain!" the dwarf protested.

"I don't want to any more than you do, Ivan, but we can't lead whoever that is to Makon." Stubbornness brought a sterner cast to Edge's features. He looked at Jerusha wordlessly.

Jerusha sensed his tension and felt grief that it should be so. She had learned to admire Edge over the brief time they had been together. Although she disagreed with some of his ideas, she wanted him to succeed, not only for his sake but for herself and for the others who had joined the crew of the *Daystar.* Desperately she searched for an answer and at last said, "Captain, just don't do anything rash. It's usually not a good idea to make a decision when we're upset, and you're very upset."

"Never mind my being upset!" Edge stalked from the bridge.

As he passed through the portal with his back straight, anger in every line of his body, Ivan stroked his chin. "I've never seen the captain like this." The man's fingers were lean and delicate, and they fluttered in the air as he waved his arms around emotionally. He was obviously very disturbed too, and the frustration that was in him came through to Jerusha in strong waves. "We've got to do something!"

"Yes, we have to," she said. "Ivan, you stay here and let me see if I can come up with something."

"Somebody *better* come up with something!" Again he looked at the screen. "If that's Sir Richard Irons out there, I'd rather be caught by rebel Cronians than by him. He's nothing but a blasted pirate!"

Jerusha left the chief engineer working fretfully over the engines and lashing out at anybody who got close to him. The old-style phase inducers kept Petroski from using the full potential of the new Mark V Star Drive engines.

She walked slowly along the corridor, her head down, and for nearly two hours roamed the ship. She went into every part of it. She watched the crew members at work. She got a rather fierce look from Tara Jaleel, but she was accustomed to that. The woman had a spirit of fiery antagonism that almost leaped out of her. She seemingly had been born angry.

Gradually, an idea began to come to Jerusha. She did not know what it was at first. Often she did not know where her ideas or feelings or senses—whatever they were—came from. With a frown on her face, she paced back and forth through the *Daystar*, thinking, thinking.

Something on this ship, or someone, seemed to be trying to tell her something. *How could this bucket of worn-out bolts tell anybody anything?* she thought as she headed forward down the central corridor and slowly entered the main computer cabin.

Fine-tuning the input circuit boards, Heck looked toward Jerusha from the sensor array console. "Couldn't stay away from me, could you?"

Ignoring his oversized ego, Jerusha was all business. "Heck, is there anything about the sensor array that could be giving us away?" She scanned the computer consoles as she crossed the cabin to him.

"What do you mean?"

"What I mean, Mr. Electronics Genius, is there a possibility that the main sensor or deflector arrays are leaking emissions that the 'shadow' can track?"

Waving her over to the console, Heck pointed to the new circuitry that he had installed a couple of days ago. "I already thought of that possibility. I installed ultrahigh-frequency redundancy chips—one to the main sensor array and the other to the deflector array. Each array monitors the other. I've programmed the main computer to alert us to any emission leakage or unusual frequency discharges."

"All that sounds wonderful . . . but you still haven't answered my question," Jerusha pursued.

Heck pursed his lips and shook his head. "The answer is yes—and no."

"*Heck!*" Jerusha's nostrils flared. She gave him a look that told him he'd better get to the point quickly.

"I've been monitoring these gauges for the last two days. Nothing out of the ordinary has happened. But even I have to leave this cabin sometime. I usually am only gone for five minutes. This morning, I went to get something to drink from the galley. Well, I forgot my cup, so I walked back to the console and bent down to pick it up. At that moment I noticed that each gauge spiked above range for a split second, then returned to normal." A puzzled look came into Heck's blue eyes as he glanced at Jerusha. "But no warning light flashed on the main computer!"

Jerusha looked at the circuit board that Heck had been working on. "So what are you working on now?"

"To my knowledge, there are no devices aboard *Daystar* that emit frequencies higher than this equipment can monitor." Heck picked up a tuning adjuster from the table and focused it on one of the new chips he had installed. "I'm adjusting the frequency mode to a much higher range." He laid the instrument back down. "Now, this should alert us if another spike occurs." He picked up a towel and wiped his face. "I sure am thirsty."

"Heck, go get yourself something from the galley. I'll baby-sit the monitor while you're gone," Jerusha volunteered.

"I'll be back in a few minutes. I want to load up on some grub too." Heck's bright smile returned to his face.

After he left the computer cabin and started down the corridor, both sensor gauges spiked for an instant. If Jerusha hadn't been looking directly at them, she would have missed it. A red warning light began flashing on the computer console!

I have to give Heck credit—as much as I hate to!

Heck ambled back into the computer room with an armload of food. Seeing the warning light flashing, he laid down his feast on a side table. "It spiked again, didn't it? And this time we got an alert."

"Congratulations on a job well done. Now, we just have to figure out where it's coming from," Jerusha said as she picked up a synthetic fruit packet and opened it.

Heck shrugged his shoulders. "It's not going to be *that* easy." He twisted the cap off his drink. "The spike is too fast and unpredictable. I can tell you *when* it happens, but I'm a light-year away from telling you anything else."

"Keep working on it," Jerusha exhorted him as she left the computer room.

Heck took a big bite from his sandwich.

Jerusha had intended to pass the galley and inspect navigations, then decided to go in after all and get a quick bite to eat. She picked up a tray, chose black coffee and a chicken sandwich, and sat down at a table.

At another table, Dai Bando and two grunt crewmen were quickly downing their food as Studs Cagney bellowed their next work assignments at them. At still another table, other grunts were eating, no doubt glad that Studs seemed particularly interested in Dai.

Something's wrong in here. I can't tell what it is —but something's not right. Jerusha felt this as she bit into her sandwich.

Studs waved his arm at the grunts and Dai, signaling them that it was time to get back to work.

As Dai passed Jerusha, he smiled and winked. "Any luck with the shadow?"

Jerusha returned his smile. "I think we're getting closer, but we really need a breakthrough soon."

Studs Cagney came up to Dai and snorted. "You can visit on your own time, grunt. Now get moving!"

Dai grinned again and waved at Jerusha. "See you later!"

Jerusha nodded at him as he left, whistling an old song. When they were gone from the galley, she noticed that her uncomfortable impression lessened in intensity. She took a deep breath and continued forward toward navigations, which was located just behind the bridge.

On the way she encountered Ringo. His brow was contracted into lines. He looked worried, almost afraid.

"Have we been able to shake off that shadow?" he asked her.

"No. Not yet, Ringo."

"We've got to get away from whoever that is. Probably it's Irons," he said in frustration.

"Yes, we do. But it's not easy. It's possible that Irons might have a faster ship than the *Daystar.* And Ivan says we can't engage full power on the Star Drive engines. He's very frustrated with the phase inducers."

Something like pain crossed Ringo's face, and Jerusha put out her hand and rested it on his shoulder. "Don't worry, Ringo. We'll make it."

"Will we?" He looked at her despairingly. "I've failed at everything I've ever done, Jerusha. Just one time in my life I'd like to do something right."

"You *haven't* failed at everything. Nobody has failed at everything."

"Sure I have. I grew up in an orphanage. I never knew who my parents were. All I know of my background is this . . ." He pulled the medallion from beneath his tunic and held it up. It was made of gold and had the picture of a hawk on one side with writing below that read: *Fortibus Fortuna Adiuvat.* Turning it over, he said, "I suppose this could be my father, but I have no idea—and I can't read this writing."

That side of the coin revealed the profile of a very strong-looking man. But Jerusha could not read the words underneath, either.

Slipping the medallion back under his tunic, Ringo said, "I was always smaller than the other guys and not as smart—except in computers. I thought I had it made when I got into the Academy, but then I washed out there."

"So did the rest of us. That wasn't your fault. The commander didn't like any of us. She didn't like anyone who was different."

Ringo looked at her anxiously. "But I *did* fail. You see, I haven't done anything right. I thought this trip might be different. I thought we could find Makon and find that tridium and then we could say we'd done something."

Jerusha felt compassion for the boy. To her he was like a younger brother. Even though she was only a year older, she felt herself much more mature. "It'll be all right, Ringo," she said warmly and smiled at him. "Just hang in there."

Jerusha made her way to the captain's cabin next, and when the door opened to her knock, she stepped inside. As she had expected, Edge was at his desk, which was cluttered as always. He was staring down at some papers, and when he glanced up, his frustration seemed to leap out at her. "Well, what is it this time?"

"Captain," Jerusha said quietly, "I think I've found something."

"Found what?" He got to his feet, walked around the table, and took her arm. "What is it, Jerusha? Something we can use?"

"I think so," she said, aware of his hand holding her tightly. "You're hurting my arm," she said. "I'm not going to run away."

"Oh—sorry! I guess I'm just upset." Edge dropped his hand and clenched his fingers together. "Well, what is it?"

"I've been going over the ship, and, Captain, something is *wrong*."

"You mean with the engines or the Star Drive?"

"No. I don't mean with the ship itself. I mean something is wrong with some person. Some member of the crew."

"Well, we have a pretty rough crew. But you know your own people, and you've had a chance to meet the original crew members. Who do you—what do you mean, something's wrong?"

Jerusha felt frustrated. "I can't explain it, sir," she said. "It's just like when a musician hears a piece and there's just one note off-key. Others, who aren't musicians, may not hear it, but he knows it. There's something rotten on board the *Daystar*, and it doesn't have anything to do with the electronics or the weapons systems or the Star Drive. There's something wrong with a *person*. I'm sure of it."

Ruffling his hair nervously, Edge said, "But you could say that about any crew. We're not angels on board this ship. At least I'm not."

"Nor am I, but I believe someone is badly out of step with what's going on."

Edge paced the cabin, his head down. He made a strong shape as he moved, his shoulders broad, his waist narrow. There was a catlike element about him, smoothly graceful, that Jerusha admired. Finally he said, "Well, what do you want to do? I suppose you have a plan."

"Yes, sir, I have. Let me talk to each member of the crew individually. But you'll have to give the order. I don't have that authority."

"Each member of the crew? What for?"

"If I can get in a room and talk with them individually, I may be able to pick up on something. Of course, as you say, we all have our problems, and I'll have to sort them out. But this is a *very* bad thing, Captain Edge."

Edge threw up his hands. "All right. Let's do it." He sat down. "You can start with me. Find out if I'm the villain."

Jerusha laughed softly. "I know you're not the villain. You're not always the smartest man in the world, but you're not bad."

"What do you mean, I'm not the smartest man in the world?" Edge demanded. "I always thought I was."

"Yes, I realize that. You're *awfully* conceited."

"Well, I've got a lot to be conceited about." Edge tried to lighten the moment. Then he said, "All right, Jerusha. I'll give the order, and we'll hope that you come up with something right away, or we'll have to give up."

Jerusha looked across the low table into the face of Tara Jaleel. She was met with a cool, resistant stare from the Masai woman.

"What's this all about?" Jaleel demanded. "I don't know what the captain means—why should we all have to have an interview with *you*. Are you some kind of a shrink?"

"No," Jerusha said. "It's just that sometimes I'm . . . well . . . able to understand things about people. And that can be helpful, especially when a group must work together."

"Well, what do you understand about me?" Jaleel's words were spoken roughly, and she kept her back straight.

"I feel you have to work pretty hard at that tough act of yours to cover up a heart that's not all that bad."

"What would you know about my heart? You're just a child!"

"I'm not as old as you are, Tara, but I know one thing. Anybody that stays angry constantly like you do is headed for trouble."

"I can handle any trouble that comes my way."

"I'm sure you could handle any physical trouble with weapons or hand-to-hand, but there are other kinds of trouble."

Tara Jaleel frowned at the girl across from her. At first she had had contempt for all the Junior Space Rangers, but she had learned that most of them were able to do their jobs. Jerusha was the leader. She had recognized that at once. As now she studied the smooth features of the ensign's squarish face, she saw eyes that met hers unblinkingly.

Jaleel was not a woman who shared her feelings—or even admitted she had them—and it embarrassed her to know that this mere child who sat so calmly before her was understanding her so well. Angrily she slammed her fist on the table. "I don't have to stand for this! Say what you have to say!"

"I don't have anything further to say. You may go when you're ready, Tara."

Jaleel got to her feet and walked to the door stiffly. When she got there she turned back and said, "I know what you're doing. You're trying to find out if there are any troublemakers on the crew. I suppose you've got me down for one."

"No," Jerusha Ericson said quietly. "You only make trouble for yourself, Tara, with your hard ways. But I pray that someday you'll change."

Stunned by the reply, Tara Jaleel eyed Jerusha. Finally she said in a voice that was almost a sneer, "That's fine. You just keep on praying, but don't cross me! You hear me, Ensign?"

"I hear you, Tara."

The door closed quietly behind Tara Jaleel, and Jerusha mentally crossed out another name. "Well, she's tough and could be rather unpleasant under certain circumstances, but she's honest. She's not a traitor."

Getting up wearily, Jerusha stretched, for she had

spent hours talking to crew members. She had eliminated all of her own crew—she knew they had no reason for wanting to sabotage the ship. Her interview with Ivan had been brief. He was open, not difficult to understand. Zeno Thrax was a different matter. If there was anyone *able* to sabotage the cruiser, it would be the albino. He was the first officer and knew the ship better than anyone except Edge himself. But what was going on inside the man, Jerusha couldn't tell. The interview with him had gone on for a long time.

"I just don't know about the first officer," she told Bronwen Llewellen. "He may be the one. I can't get any impressions of what he's really like. He's built a wall around himself. He *seems* like a good man, but who knows with a mind like that?"

Bronwen had listened quietly. "Just be very careful, Jerusha. There are dangerous things on this ship. Wicked things. And wickedness in a man or a woman can be more deadly than a stray meteorite or a space pirate."

Contessa came over and put her head on Jerusha's lap. Jerusha stroked the broad forehead and looked down into the liquid brown eyes. "Now, you're not a traitor, are you, Contessa?" The dog whined, and her tail beat on the floor.

Jerusha sat there for a time after Bronwen left her, then said wearily, "Well, I've got to interview the rest of the crew. Maybe the problem is all in my mind—and Bronwen's—" she said to herself, "but I've got to find out."

She talked with several of the crew members under Studs Cagney's authority. Finally she interviewed the crew chief himself.

He came in, sat down in front of her, and leaned across the table. "What do you want?" he demanded.

Jerusha gazed at him thoughtfully. He was a rough-looking individual. His face was scarred from past brawls. He was obviously a heavy drinker, and she could smell alcohol on him now. But there were plenty of tough men—and women as well—at the Space Academy, though none looked quite as rough as Cagney.

"I just wanted to talk to you about the ship and about our mission."

"Our mission," Cagney sneered, "doesn't amount to anything. Can't run a ship with infants and grandmas."

Contessa got up suddenly, lowered her head, and began advancing on Cagney. A growl started in her throat.

Instantly Cagney put himself in a defensive position. "Keep that dog off me!"

"She's not going to hurt you. Lie down, Contessa." Jerusha waited, and the dog moved to her feet but did not lie down. Something in the dog's attitude alarmed Jerusha.

But she began speaking quietly with Cagney, asking questions about the *Daystar*, trying to pick up some signal. And before long, she was convinced she had found her man. It was not just that Studs Cagney was rough and crude. There was something else— something devious, something even violent. That came across, finally, after her general questions about the cruiser had lulled him into a sort of security.

This is the one, she thought. She reached down to her belt and touched the button on her communicator, then said, "Captain, would you come to my cabin, please?"

Studs sat up straighter, his eyes widening. "What do you want the captain for?"

Jerusha did not answer. She suddenly knew that this was a dangerous man indeed!

The door opened, and Edge walked in. "What's this all about?" he demanded.

"This is your man, Captain." Jerusha turned and faced Cagney. "He's the one who is betraying this ship."

Cagney's face grew red. "What are you talking about? I ain't no traitor!"

"I think you'd better search his cabin. Go through his things carefully," Jerusha said calmly. "I wouldn't be surprised if he hasn't been sending a signal to that shadow that's on our trail."

"You ain't going to listen to this kid, are you, Captain?"

Mark Edge looked at the crewman's face. He'd always had confidence in Cagney's ability to keep the crew in line and to do the rough work. But he was troubled by something that he saw in the eyes of the burly crew chief. "I think we'd better have a look at your things, Studs. If you are innocent, we won't find anything."

Cagney began to bluster, and when the captain ignored him, he shouted, "You're not lookin' at my stuff!" He headed for the door.

Jerusha cried, "Stop him, Captain!"

Edge grabbed Cagney's arm. It was like seizing a piece of oak, and he was unable to avoid the blow that came at him from nowhere. He felt himself going down, and stars flickered before his eyes as a sharp pain hit him in the temple.

"Contessa! Hold!"

Cagney, on the way to the door, suddenly whirled. The dog was advancing on him, her eyes gleaming and her lips drawn back to reveal a fearsome row of white teeth. He drew a Neuromag from his belt and aimed it at the dog. He never pulled the trigger, though, for the dog leaped quicker than thought and fastened her teeth on his wrist. Cagney yelled and began to fight the dog, and the weapon dropped to the floor.

Edge rolled to his feet. He snatched up the sidearm, checked the setting, and aimed. He pressed the trigger, and there was a slight humming sound. A blue light emanated from the end of the Neuromag and enveloped Studs Cagney. At once his eyes rolled up, and he fell loosely to the floor, collapsing as if he were boneless.

"Hold, Contessa!" Jerusha commanded again. The dog stepped back, keeping her teeth bared, and Jerusha turned to the captain. "I rather think all that proves we've found our man."

"I believe so. I'm going to keep him here. You get Ringo and Heck and go search his things."

Jerusha summoned the two boys and informed them as to what had happened.

Heck said, "I'll bet he's the one. Come on. Let's see if he's got anything in his stuff."

It took only a brief search to find a small black box. Heck picked it up and said, "Here it is. Some kind of transmitter." He handed it to Ringo, who looked it over.

"This appears to be the new homing device used by the Intergalactic Rangers. Look, it's got a powerful sender. Maybe we ought to throw it away," Ringo said.

"No, don't do that," Jerusha said. "Maybe we can use it to throw them off our trail. Let's go back and show it to the captain."

The three went back and found that Studs Cagney was sitting pale-faced under the Neuromag in the captain's hand.

"We found this, sir," Jerusha said. "Ringo and Heck say it's a powerful homing device that can send our position to almost anywhere."

Edge took a look, then said, "Well, what do you have to say for yourself, Cagney?"

Cagney glared at the three with hatred, then shrugged his muscular shoulders. "All right. I done it. So what?"

"*Why* did you do it, Studs?" Mark Edge asked quietly. Jerusha knew he had trusted this man and was disappointed, as always, when someone failed him.

"For money, that's for what!"

"Who paid you off? Was it Sir Richard Irons?"

"I ain't tellin' that. You can kill me if you want to, but I don't squeal."

"I don't think we'll have to kill you. Irons is the only one who knows what I'm doing." Handing the sidearm to Ringo, Edge said, "Cagney is under arrest. We'll keep him locked up in his cabin. See to it, will you, Smith?"

"Yes, sir," Ringo said. He waved the Neuromag. "Come on, you. You're going to jail."

After the door closed behind the two, Heck said, "That's gonna put a hole in the crew. We can't trust him anymore, Captain."

"We'll just have to muddle through. The first thing is to get rid of our 'shadow.'"

"That won't be hard now, sir," Jerusha said. "We can send them a false signal and then slip away while they're following it."

"That's a good idea. I'm glad I thought of it." Heck nodded happily. "Let's call a meeting and tell them what we've decided."

Both the captain and Jerusha smiled at the impudence of Heck Jordan.

"I think I'll remain as captain of the *Daystar* just a little longer, Heck. But I'll keep you in mind when I start looking for a replacement for myself. Come on, both of you. We've got work to do!"

8
Dai Bando Takes a Stand

W hat we ought to do is shuck him out the door into space!"

Those crew members who were not on duty were gathered around the mess table to discuss the case of Studs Cagney. Edge, watching from the head of the table, saw that the newcomers had arranged themselves on one side—Ringo Smith, Heck Jordan, Raina St. Clair, and Mei-Lani Lao. Jerusha Ericson, Dai Bando, and Bronwen Llewellen sat close together.

On the other side of the table, Ivan Petroski, Zeno Thrax, and Tara Jaleel had ranked themselves.

The argument had been going on for some time, and again Jaleel's voice rose. "There's no question about it. He needs to be executed."

"That's a little bit harsh, isn't it?" Bronwen Llewellen suggested. The gentleness in the older woman contrasted almost violently with the antagonism in the face of the weapons officer.

"He's a traitor!" Lieutenant Jaleel snapped. "He could have led every one of us to our deaths!"

"Perhaps. We don't know that," Mei-Lani said gently. She was the youngest in the room, and usually her shyness prevented her from speaking. There was pleading in her voice as she said, "Perhaps he deserves a second chance."

"He's had a second chance and a third," Tara Jaleel said. "You don't know him like I do. Why, he's done enough to be executed for, even if he hadn't betrayed us to Sir Richard Irons! I vote to cast him into space!"

Captain Edge had a brief vivid thought about what it would be like to be jettisoned into space. It would be a quick death, but still, there was something about being shoved out into the void. Your body would float forever . . .

Heck looked around and said, "If we're going to vote, I vote we ex him out!"

"There must certainly be an accounting for what Cagney has done, but you're very careless with life, Heck," Raina said. She was wearing the standard uniform, which the captain insisted on—white tunic, close-fitting maroon trousers, black half boots with rubber soles. "Haven't you ever made a mistake? Haven't you ever done anything that you needed to be shown mercy for?"

"Now, wait a minute!" Heck protested. "*I'm* not on trial here! *I'm* not the one who betrayed us!"

"You may have done something else just as bad," Raina said. "Most of us have."

"Have you, Ensign St. Clair?" Zeno Thrax asked suddenly, his colorless eyes fixed on Raina. His skin was so pale that he made the rest of the crew look almost dark by comparison. Then he said, "Isn't there something in your Christianity to remove what you call sin?"

Raina flushed as all eyes went to her. "Yes, there is, sir. We are forgiven for sin when we turn to Jesus Christ."

"You have spoken of Him before," Thrax said, interest in his face. "I fail to understand how one man dying can help anyone else. He couldn't even help Himself."

"But He could have," Raina said. "Our Bible teaches

us that Jesus could have asked His Father and He would have sent legions of angels."

This seemed to fascinate Thrax. He leaned forward even further and locked his gaze onto that of Raina St. Clair. "And why didn't His 'Father' send 'legions of angels'?"

"Because Jesus and His Father, God, had agreed that since sin had come into the human race, someone had to die to cleanse people of it."

"Ah, human sacrifice," Thrax said. "It takes place in many cultures—in my own for one. Every year we would select one of our number and take him out and execute him."

"But that one you executed was a sinner himself. He couldn't die for the sins of anyone else," Raina explained. "Jesus was a perfect man, actually God Himself, and that's why He could die for the sins of the world."

"Just a minute!" Ivan Petroski said. "We're not here to talk religion! We've got to decide what to do with a traitor!"

"That's what we are doing," Raina said quickly. "The Bible teaches us that even the worst of men can be redeemed through the blood of Jesus."

The captain felt out of his depth. He said, "We can't turn this into a seminar on religion. We've got to decide what to do."

Mei-Lani said, "I agree that Studs Cagney *must* be held accountable for what he has done. But, Captain, there are two kinds of people in this world—those who show mercy and those who show none. When you go back through the history of the world, you see that most men, and most women, are of the second kind. Is it not possible for us to show mercy in this case?"

The captain interrupted. "I'm sorry, Mei-Lani, but all that is neither here nor there."

Dai Bando, who had thus far said absolutely nothing, spoke up then. "Captain, I'm not really a member of the crew. I'm just—just a grunt. But can I say something?"

"Of course, Dai. What is it?" Edge said quickly. He did not think the boy would have much of importance to say. But at least while he spoke, Edge could be racking his brain, trying to figure a way out of this problem.

Dai was not seated at the table. He had been leaning against the wall, listening. Even in repose there was something athletic and graceful about him. His dark hair and eyes formed a startling contrast with the white wall behind him. "Look, I know that Chief Cagney has done serious wrong, and all of you know he has been no friend to me." He spoke slowly but with certainty.

Everybody knew that Cagney had given Dai the worst, dirtiest jobs that could be found on the spaceship and used him cruelly without actually laying hands on him. A crew chief could make life miserable for anyone in his crew, and Studs had certainly done so with Dai.

Speaking a little more rapidly now, Dai said, "But it's like Raina says. All of us have done something wrong. Maybe something worse than Studs. I know I wouldn't want everybody here to know about everything I've done."

"You never betrayed your comrades, did you?" Tara Jaleel snapped. "It's not like he was an enemy in another force! He was one of us! That's worse! An enemy can be honorable, but there's nothing honorable about a traitor!"

"I don't claim that there is," Dai said earnestly. "But I agree with Raina and Mei-Lani that, in this case, it seems the man deserves another chance." He looked at the captain. "Besides, it's going to be hard for you to run the ship without a crew chief, isn't it?"

That had been bothering Captain Edge considerably. He nodded, and his lips grew thin. "You're right about that. Studs knows things about the ship that most of the rest of us don't know. He may be a traitor, but he's a thumping good crew chief."

"Well, what about this?" Dai said. "I'm not trying to promote myself, but if you would let Cagney continue doing his work, I'll stand for him."

"What does that mean, you'll *stand* for him?" Tara Jaleel snapped. "How can you 'stand for' another person?"

"I'll be responsible for him," Dai said. "I'll watch him every minute of the day and night. As the captain will tell you, my reflexes are fairly good. I've learned a little bit about the ship—not much, but I think I can keep him from doing anything damaging—at least I'll try. That way you wouldn't lose his crew chief abilities, Captain."

A murmur went around the table, and Captain Edge saw that there still were divided opinions. Jaleel, of course, was for throwing him out the hatch right away—Petroski, too, probably. But of the younger members, only Heck Jordan seemed to have this kind of attitude.

Finally Edge made a decision. "All right, Dai. For the time being I'm putting you in charge of the man. Remember, he's treacherous. He's proven that, hasn't he? And if he gives you one minute's trouble—if he starts destroying the ship or doing *anything* to cause trouble—you put him down."

Dai studied the captain, then said, "If I see anything like that, I'll put him *out*. I can guarantee that."

"You can have Contessa to help you," Jerusha said. "She's got more sense than lots of people, and she'll be good to keep an eye on him."

"All right. It's settled then." Edge got up. "I'll be expecting a good report." He paused, then said, "Those of you who are advocating mercy have won this round, but it will be up to Cagney. One false step, and out the hatch he goes."

"Good!" Tara Jaleel said. "You watch. That man's no good. He won't make it."

Studs Cagney squinted at Dai Bando, and there was puzzlement on his scarred face. For two days, ever since they had shaken off the ship that had followed them, Cagney had gone about his normal duties. The captain had warned him sternly that one false move and he would be turned over to Tara Jaleel. "You know," the captain said, "what *she'll* do to you."

Studs Cagney had known, indeed, what the weapons officer would do. He had seen her do it before to men, and it was not pleasant to contemplate.

Now, staring at the dark-haired boy who worked beside him, he ran over in his mind the events that had taken place.

Dai Bando had confronted him as soon as the captain turned Studs over to him, saying, "Chief, I hope we get along. I put in a good word for you with the captain, but I also told him if you try anything out of line, I'll break your neck."

Looking at the boy, Studs knew that Dai Bando was perfectly capable of doing that. He had seen the tremendous strength and the almost supernatural quickness of the young man. *The only way to stop him is with a Neuromag on full,* he'd said to himself. But he had no weapon, nor would he have access to any, and even if he did eliminate Dai Bando, there would still be the others. So he had sullenly gone to work.

96

"Where do you come from, Studs?" Dai asked. "I mean, where's your home?"

"What difference does it make?"

"I guess you've led a pretty adventurous life. You've been on lots of trips like this, haven't you?"

"More than you could count. I was at 'em before you were born."

"I'd like to hear about some of them. This is my first trip, and I'm green as grass."

The young man's cheerful attitude gave the burly crew chief pause. It was almost impossible to stay angry at Dai. Studs had tried his best to humiliate the boy, to make life miserable for him, but always he was greeted by a cheerful smile.

Cagney said, "Do you really care where I've been and what I've done?"

"Why, sure, Chief. I like to hear about far-off places, and I guess you've been about everywhere."

Studs scrutinized him, trying to decide if this was flattery. But Dai was working on the bulkhead and was whistling under his breath. He had a fine singing voice, and from time to time would break out into an old song, sometimes using words that Studs could not understand.

"Well, if you're really interested," Cagney said, "I did make a trip a few years back to the planet Zimgo. That was a pretty hairy time—even for me."

He launched into the story, and before long the two were sitting down, Studs spreading his hands as he spun his tale and Dai on a box in front of him, listening with rapt attention.

"Well, that's how we got out of it," Cagney said, "but I didn't think we was going to."

Dai took a deep breath. "Boy, I don't see how you did all that, Studs. I don't think anybody else could have done it."

Nobody had ever given Studs Cagney a great deal of appreciation. He had grown up the hard way and had gotten rougher. But this boy seated before him fascinated him. He knew that, indeed, Dai Bando had gone to bat for him with the captain. "Why'd you tell the captain you'd look out for me?"

"Well, in the first place, I didn't think we could run the ship without you."

The answer pleased the crew chief. "You're mighty right you couldn't. Have to turn around and go back. I'm the one that keeps this thing pulled together. What's the other reason?"

"Well, I just hate to see anybody's life wasted."

"What do you mean, 'wasted'?"

"I mean, if Tara Jaleel threw you out the door, you'd be wasted, wouldn't you?"

A shiver went over Studs, for he knew that Jaleel would do exactly that. "I reckon that's right enough," he said. He thought for a moment and said, "Did you hear all that talking that girl does, that Raina St. Clair?"

"Sure, I heard it."

"All that stuff about Jesus and one man dying for the sins of somebody else?"

"Yeah, that's right. That's what she believes."

"Do you believe it?"

Dai Bando nodded. "Yes, I believe it. I've been a believer a long time. My aunt is a believer, too. She's the best Christian I know."

"You mean the navigator?"

"Sure." Dai Bando's face glowed with a sudden flush. "She's a great person. She'd do anything for anybody. Always sees the best in people."

"Well, I never heard of such a thing—one person dying for another!"

Dai Bando began to talk about Jesus Christ. He did so easily and naturally, but finally he laughed in embarrassment. "I didn't mean to preach you a sermon, Studs."

Studs Cagney ordinarily would have exploded if anyone had tried to tell him he needed religion, but the things that had come into his life lately and his close brush with death had made him think. "Oh, I guess it's all right for old women and young folks. It's too late for me, though."

Dai Bando suddenly looked very serious. "It's never too late when a man wants to change. God's always ready. But there I go again. Sorry."

Studs turned back to his work, his face a study in concentration. "Maybe sometime we can talk about Jesus again, huh, Dai?"

"Sure, Studs. Anytime you'd like. As a matter of fact, we're going to have a service. I wish you'd come."

"You mean a preachin' service?"

"That's right. My aunt likes to do that, you know. She's better than most preachers. I'm sure she'd be glad to have you. Just be a small group of us, though."

"They wouldn't want me."

"I want you," Dai said.

"You do?" True amazement flickered across the tough face of Studs Cagney. He could not understand this. Force and violence and hatred had been his life, and now this new thing leaping out at him confused him. "I wouldn't want to do a thing like that. That's for women."

"Nope. It's for me, and I'm not a woman."

Studs thought for a while. "Maybe I'll go just once."

"Fine. We'll be glad to have you."

9
Ringo Fails the Test

The trip through space was a delight to Dai Bando. Never having been more than a hundred feet off the ground (in the top of a tall pine tree), he found the voyage both exciting and a little frightening.

On *Daystar*'s bridge, the stars raced by the ship like thousands of tiny comets. He knew that the Star Drive engines produced this effect. Ivan, Ringo, and Heck had figured out a way to strengthen the phase inducers, enabling the Mark V Star Drive to come to full speed. Dai also knew that stars did travel through space, though from earth they appeared motionless. As he looked forward, Dai kept expecting one of the stars to come crashing straight into the ship.

"You still worried we're going to crash into a star?" Bronwen asked, as she walked onto the bridge. She smiled at the look on his face.

"Aunt Bronwen, I just can't get over how fast the stars are traveling. They must be going a million miles per hour."

"Will you stop it!" She gave him a hug. "One of the things that make star navigation rather easy is that the stars are relatively stationary. Their journey through space takes thousands and thousands of millennia."

"That's not what it looks like to me," he admitted sheepishly.

Bronwen gave her nephew a slight shove, then walked to the front of the bridge and looked into space. "Don't trust your eyes. It's *Daystar* that's traveling many times the speed of light. And the stars are many millions of miles from each other. The distances are quite incredible! Our navigational computer has plenty of time to guide us around them. This ship is the fastest one I've ever been on, but she's not so fast that the navigational computer will lose control of her. Now, *relax!*"

A few days later, the voyage to Makon was over. Looking out the porthole, Dai Bando was examining with delight the planet that lay just before them. It seemed to grow larger as they drew closer. He said to Ringo, who was watching with him, "This is really exciting, isn't it?"

Ringo had been on several interstellar missions while an ensign at the Academy. He affected his voice to sound like an old hand. "Oh, I suppose so—to one who's never been on a voyage before."

Actually Ringo was thrilled, as always, for he loved to travel in space, but he wanted to seem cool. Dai excelled him in so many things that he felt intimidated. Now it was *his* turn to be the expert. "We'll be coming in for a landing now. We'll need to brace ourselves for it."

Dai Bando looked down at the dull gray globe. "It's a pretty bad-looking place," he said. "I expected it to be green and look a little like Earth."

"Well, the galaxy's full of planets, and none of them are exactly alike."

Ringo looked downward, and he too thought that Makon was an inhospitable-looking planet, to say the least. There were bodies of water, and here and there spots of green, but mostly the landscape looked like desert. The high country was bald, without any enticing greenery at all. "Not a place where I'd want to come and live," he said. "Well, get ready. We're coming in for the landing."

On the bridge, Capt. Mark Edge began landing instructions. "Edge to crew," he announced on the intercom. "We're entering the outer atmosphere of Makon, so it's going to get a little shaky. All hands secure at your stations."

The ship began to vibrate as the atmospheric gases thickened and *Daystar* started her descent. Soon the stabilizers and wings provided lift for the ship as she neared the planet's surface.

Makon was much larger than Earth—almost the size of Jupiter. The planet had three giant mountain ranges separated by vast deserts. Edge had visited only one mountain. It was inhabited by the race of human beings that called themselves the Dulkins.

Captain Edge yelled back at his navigator. "Llewellen, have you finished plotting the course?"

Without taking her eyes off of her navigational console, Bronwen answered evenly, "Lay in a course 245 mark 123. This will bring us to the mountain range you indicated."

Daystar flew gracefully over a red desert range that seemed as vast as space itself. A few minutes more passed before Captain Edge announced over the intercom, "Land ho!"

Edge guided the ship in a circle around a huge mountain that was mostly dark gray rock topped with a spectacular snowcap.

Raina, who had been monitoring communications, said excitedly, "That mountain must be twenty times higher than Mount Everest!" Her eyes were as big as silver dollars.

"Twenty-two times to be exact," Captain Edge

confirmed. "The mountains are higher and the continents much larger than anything on earth. The gravity is much stronger as well. I believe that's what makes the tridium harder than Earth's diamonds." He adjusted the helm controls to lower the ship to the surface just south of the mountain.

When the spaceship came to a complete halt, Captain Edge exhaled a breath of relief. He turned to Jerusha, standing beside him, and said, "Well, we're here."

"Yes, sir. It was a good landing."

"Not much of a trick to landing on a level plain like this." He shrugged. "Now, I want to get this mission over with." He nodded to Bronwen Llewellen, who was standing off to one side. "A good job, Bronwen."

"Thank you, Captain."

Edge turned to Tara. "Lieutenant Jaleel, we'll take a squad and do a scouting mission on the surface of the planet."

The dark face of Tara Jaleel grew alert at once. "Yes, Captain." She hesitated a moment, then said, "What should I expect? Resistance?"

"I think you might have some of that," Captain Edge said. He cast a strange look at Jerusha. "When I was here the last time, some of the natives weren't too friendly—at least when I left."

"Then we may expect to do battle with them?" Jaleel asked eagerly.

"Actually, I don't want any trouble," Edge said. "Don't start anything. You should be able to protect yourselves—they have only primitive weapons. No Neuromags, just the old-fashioned gunpowder weapons. Almost like the Old West. Put on full body armor, though—and for what she's worth, take along that stupid dog. Make contact with the Dulkins. Tell them I want to have a meeting."

Disappointment swept across Lieutenant Jaleel's face. Undoubtedly she had been anticipating a rousing battle, but the captain's intentions were clear. "Yes, sir," she said.

"You'll find some difficulty out there because of the gravity. Take only the strongest of the crew with you. And remember, this is just a scouting expedition."

"Is the oxygen level satisfactory for human life?" Jaleel inquired.

"Yes, you won't need to carry oxygen. Report back as soon as you make contact. Remember, we come in peace."

"Yes, sir."

Jaleel picked her scouting expedition quickly. She included Jerusha, Dai Bando, Studs Cagney, three of Studs's working crew, and, to his surprise, Ringo Smith.

She called them all together and passed out weapons. The Neuromags were oval in shape and fit into the palm of the hand. Three lights (blue—stun; red—heat; yellow—kill) indicated the power settings. The unit had a thumb switch trigger that could be programmed to operate universally or with only an assigned thumbprint.

"The captain has ordered that we do no harm to the natives. He wants a peaceful meeting. When we're outside, I want us to spread out. But stay in contact with each other. Keep your communicators on. Remember, do them no harm."

Studs stared at her. "What if they try to kill *us?*"

"They have only primitive weapons," Jaleel said. "And we're wearing full body armor."

Ringo glanced around. He felt uncertain and a little afraid. He also had the feeling that Jaleel had chosen him for this expedition just to show up his inadequacies. She knew he was not good at physical things, and he knew that what lay ahead would be more physical than operating a computer.

They moved along to the equipment room where each donned full body armor. Then they followed Lieutenant Jaleel to the portal, where she spoke into the voice lock. They watched the door slide silently into its sheath, and then they followed her out.

The first thing Ringo did when he set foot on the surface of Makon was to fall flat. The gravity was like a hundred-pound weight pressing him down.

"Get off the ground, Smith!" Jaleel said.

"Yes, Lieutenant!" Ringo struggled to his feet, embarrassed.

He saw that the others had no trouble at all. But, of course, Studs was a muscular man, and Jaleel was one of the strongest women he had ever seen. Dai Bando, he saw, walked as easily as if there were no gravity. Jerusha seemed to move effortlessly. He noted that even Contessa was so strong that the gravity seemed to have little effect on her. She went running to Jerusha's side, and Jerusha murmured, "Down, girl," as the animal attempted to rear up.

Ringo wished he were back inside the ship.

"All right. Spread out. Ensign Ericson, you take that side of the line. I'll take this side. The rest of you keep positioned in the middle. Now, let's get this done."

Ringo felt very much alone on the surface of the barren planet as the others pulled away and left him. Soon Studs Cagney, who was to his right, and Dai Bando, on his left, disappeared behind the broken rock. The ground was uneven, and as he struggled along, lifting each foot with effort, he tried to avoid the potholes and cracks in the surface. There were patches of unhealthy-looking gray grass and something that looked like cactus, which he carefully avoided. There were no signs of animal life for a time, but finally he saw movement over to his right, and a creature looking like a wolf appeared, then disappeared.

Fingering his weapon, Ringo nervously hoped they didn't meet any deadly life-forms. On the planet Terraa, he had been almost killed by a flying creature with leatherlike wings and a faceful of razor-sharp teeth. He still had nightmares about that.

For half an hour Ringo trudged along before having to sit down and rest. He was gasping, and the dull sun overhead seemed much hotter than Earth's sun. A dry wind was blowing, which seemed to parch his face, and he pulled a flask from his belt, lifted the visor that would turn bullets, and drank eagerly. The water was tepid, but still it refreshed him.

He replaced the cap carefully and got up to move on. "I wish Jaleel had chosen somebody else," he muttered. "I'd rather be doing my job on the computer system."

Then his thoughts went to what lay ahead, and Ringo, who had a vivid imagination, began to think of what he would do if the mission were successful. *Why, I'll have more money than I ever thought about, if what Captain Edge says is true. I'll be able to buy the biggest, best computer made. Then I'll have the money to try out some of my ideas.* Ringo Smith was a dreamer.

And so as he stumbled along over the broken, rocky surface with the hot wind beating upon him, he paid little attention to what was ahead. If he had, he might have turned aside, for he might have caught a glimpse of the creature that had emerged from a hole in the earth and now was poised on top of a rocky crag overhanging the path that Ringo took.

It was a fierce-looking creature with strong, sharp talons on all four limbs. It had a face like a gorilla. The mouth was huge and bore razor-sharp fangs. The eyes were reddish, and there was a hungry expression on the creature's face as it clung to the side of the rock and looked down on its approaching prey.

The animal waited until the two-legged creature was directly beneath it. Then, with a wild screech, it flung itself down, claws extended.

Ringo, despite the gravity, leaped at the unearthly sound. He had time only to look up and could see nothing but sharp claws and white fangs. He threw up his arms defensively, forgetting the Neuromag in his belt, and was thrown to the ground by the force of the creature's body.

The animal's claws scratched deep gashes in the armor, hard as it was. The fangs bit at his visor, and he could smell the creature's foul odor. Over and over he rolled, now underneath, now on top, as the two somersaulted down a rough slope. When they reached the bottom, Ringo tried desperately to pull his sidearm from his belt, but the creature's lithe, muscular body was pressed against him. The fangs were again gnawing at the visor.

Ringo was almost paralyzed with fright. *I'm going to die*, he thought. *He's going to tear this armor off, and then he'll kill me.* Frantically he struggled, but it was hopeless. The creature was too strong. A great sadness filled him as he realized that here, at last, he had a chance to succeed at something, and now he was going to die before he could ever be a success at anything.

The creature's claw ripped through an arm of his body armor, and he felt pain like white fire. He knew it was the end.

And then—suddenly—the creature was gone! Ringo rolled over and saw a blur of motion. It was Contessa! The powerful dog had thrown herself onto the beast. The two animals now struggled, and the air was filled with the cries of the monstrous creature and the dog's deep guttural growlings and snarls as her powerful jaws snapped and tore.

Staggering to his feet, Ringo pulled at his Neuromag. He tried to aim, but the animals were so intertwined and moving so fast he could not shoot without risking hitting Contessa. Then he heard a voice calling him on his communicator, and he slapped at the button. "Quick! I've been attacked by some strange animal. Contessa's here!"

He moved closer, trying to get off a shot. But even as he watched, the beast tore free from the jaws of the big black dog and scrambled away.

Contessa followed, but suddenly a voice called out, "Contessa! Back!"

Ringo looked up to see Jerusha, who was running awkwardly in the gravity. She stopped beside Ringo and took a shot at the fleeing beast but missed, and then the awful creature disappeared down a hole.

"Are you all right, Ringo?" she asked.

"I got scratched on the arm." Ringo held out his left arm and showed the rent in the body armor. "If it hadn't been for Contessa, that thing would have killed me."

Jerusha looked down fondly and stroked the dog's head. "Good girl! Good girl!" she said. Then she turned back to Ringo. "We'd better get you to the ship. That creature's claws may have been poisonous."

Jerusha hit her communicator button and said, "Lieutenant Jaleel, Ensign Smith has been wounded by a creature. Shall I take him back for treatment to the ship?"

"Affirmative!" Jaleel's voice came sharply over the communicator. "We'll all rendezvous by the big yellow rocks. Obviously we need to stay together."

By the time Jerusha and Ringo got to the site Jaleel had mentioned, the others were there waiting.

Jaleel carelessly looked at his wound and said, "It's only a scratch."

"But the bite may have been poisonous. We don't know about these creatures," Jerusha said.

Reluctantly Jaleel said, "All right. We'll take him back to the ship, then we'll fan out in the other direction. Let's go."

They struggled along in the heavy gravity, and Ringo grew faint from loss of blood. He stumbled once, and Jaleel said sharply, "Keep up there, Smith!"

"He's hurt!" Jerusha said with indignation.

But the weapons officer had no mercy for what she called a "scratch."

"It's OK." Dai Bando moved over to Ringo and said, "Up you go." Lifting the ensign as though he were made of feathers, Dai ducked his head, and Ringo found himself straddling the boy's broad shoulders.

"You can't carry me all the way back to the ship, Dai."

"Sure I can." He winked at Jerusha. "Let's go, Ensign." He began to walk so quickly that the others had to almost run to keep up with him.

Jaleel trotted by his side, her eyes filled with something like admiration at his strength.

Cagney, despite his brawniness, seemed almost exhausted. He gasped, "You may . . . have to carry *me* . . . if we don't get . . . back pretty soon."

They were winding their way through a canyon full of razor-sharp rocks almost like coral. When they were almost through the pass, suddenly Contessa let out a sharp series of barks.

"Wait!" Jerusha said.

"We don't have time to wait!" Lieutenant Jaleel snapped.

"We'd better! Something's up there!" Jerusha warned.

Jaleel stared at her and then at the dog. "You think the dog smells something?"

"She's very alert about danger. I know her ways." Jerusha looked at the turn in the canyon ahead and said, "I think we'd better be very cautious, Lieutenant."

Jaleel looked around. "All right, Neuromags out, but set them on stun. The captain said he'd had trouble with the Dulkins before. But we want no trouble if we can help it."

They moved forward cautiously.

Ringo, still dizzy from loss of blood, drew his weapon along with the others and set it on stun. He felt Dai moving easily under him and wondered at the awesome strength of the boy.

It was Ringo who first saw the enemy. From his high position he glimpsed movement just below a bluff that rose before them. "I see them!" he said. "They're waiting for us."

Lieutenant Jaleel held up her Neuromag, and as she did, a ragged rank of Dulkins suddenly appeared. They were, Ringo saw, short and muscular. Most of them had long blackish hair and blunt features and looked to be tremendously strong, no doubt having adapted to the gravity.

"They're preparing to fire at us!" Jerusha said. "Shall we return fire, Lieutenant?"

"Not if we can help it—and get the dog back."

"Come here, Contessa," Jerusha said, and reluctantly the huge animal came to her side.

Then the sound of firing began as the Dulkins' ancient weapons exploded, followed by the thud of bullets on body armor.

The light of battle leaped into Lieutenant Jaleel's eyes. Undoubtedly she longed to return fire, but she was well aware of the captain's orders. She held her hand up and called, "We come in peace!"

Her words had no effect on the Dulkins. They surrounded the party in a wide half-circle and continued firing.

"They won't listen, Lieutenant," Cagney said. "We've got to put them down."

"All right, but be sure your weapons are on stun. We don't want anybody killed."

The Dulkins had no chance against the Neuromags. Lieutenant Jaleel was an expert shot, as was Jerusha. Their weapons sent out tiny pencil-like beams of blue light, and as soon as a ray touched one of the natives, he fell loosely to the earth. Most of the Dulkins turned and fled.

"Back to the ship," Jaleel said.

Thirty minutes later the scouting party was sitting inside the cruiser. Ringo's shirt was off and his wound had been tended by Jerusha, who had had some training in first aid. She said, "Captain, we need a *surgeon* on board."

"Well, I couldn't get one to come!" Edge snapped with irritation.

Then Lieutenant Jaleel gave her report. "If it hadn't been for the dog alerting us," she said, "we might have had more trouble than we did. Fortunately, their weapons can't penetrate the body armor."

Edge shook his head with discouragement. "I was hoping this wouldn't happen."

"Will we have to turn back?" Raina asked. Along with Mei-Lani and Heck, she was standing by the scouting party.

"No!" Captain Edge snapped. "We won't do that!"

"I don't see how we can do any mining here," Ringo said.

The captain said, "We're not going to do the mining. And all we need is a sample—just a handful of the gems to take back to Earth. We're going to make peace with the Dulkins and—"

"Well, it didn't look to me like they were going to be happy to give it to us," Cagney growled. "I think we'd better not count on any help from them."

Raina St. Clair reached out and made an adjustment on Ringo's bandage. She did not see his eyes as he turned to her. Although she was a sensitive young woman, Ringo was so withdrawn and showed his feelings so little that she had no way of knowing the affection he felt for her. She said, "I think God has brought us this far. He won't abandon us."

"It wasn't God," Jaleel said. "It was the *Daystar* that brought us here."

And Raina said no more.

"I'll have to go out and make contact with the leaders of the Dulkins myself," Captain Edge said.

"I thought you didn't leave them in a good humor," Heck Jordan said. "If they capture you, they may pull you out of that body armor and toast you on a stick."

"It may be a chance we'll have to take," Edge said quietly. He rose and said, "We can't count on their help in any case. We'll have to do some mining ourselves. It's too late today, but we'll start at first light, trying to get some samples by our own efforts. If that doesn't work, I'll have to go to the Dulkins."

113

10
Antigravity

Ow!" Heck Jordan had lifted a pick, but upon preparing to swing it, he suddenly dropped it to the ground. He spread out his hands toward Dai Bando and complained, "Look at these blisters, Dai! I can't do this kind of work another day!"

Dai, who had been swinging regularly and easily at the hard Makon surface, making the dirt fly, put down his pick and leaned against it. A fine beading of sweat covered his brow, and his chest was rising and falling with the effort of working in the heavy gravity. Nevertheless, he smiled, and his teeth looked very white against his tanned face. "You ought to wear gloves," he said.

"I ought to be working on the computer—which is what I signed up for!"

"We've got to find some samples of tridium or the whole trip's in vain," Dai said. He began to swing again, from time to time stopping to rake through what he was digging up. He worked like a machine, showing no effort, and was the despair of those with less physical strength.

Heck and Ringo, particularly, had worn blisters on their hands and developed backaches and headaches, but Edge had driven everyone hard, hoping to find samples of the ore. There had been no further sighting of the Dulkins, though from time to time a shot would ring out and often hit the body armor that they were all forced to wear.

The body armor was hot and sweaty, and Heck scratched frantically at his chest. It was useless, of course, because he could not reach his flesh, and his fingernails rasped on the armor.

"I've had enough," he told Dai. He threw down his pick and trudged off, picking up each foot with an effort. He did not look back but muttered, "I'm going to tell the captain I didn't sign on to be a slave."

When he reached the *Daystar*, he found Jerusha in the cargo room. He started to say, "I've had it with this—" Then he halted and looked down. "What in the world," he gasped, "are *those* things?"

Heck pulled off his helmet and wiped at the sweat on his face as he stared down at the strange creatures gathered around Contessa. They looked like small squirrels, except that they were striped with reddish and black lines. They kept nuzzling the dog.

Jerusha said, "I don't know. They're some sort of pups."

"Where did you get them?"

"I found them when I was out scouting today. I think they've been abandoned." She smiled. "They think Contessa's their mother."

Contessa, indeed, was acting like a mother. In turn, she nuzzled the striped furry animals as they tried to get closer to her.

Jerusha had filled several small bottles and had apparently been feeding them. "Here, help me feed these darling little creatures."

"Darling? They don't look darling to me!" Nevertheless, Heck took two bottles and two pups. The striped animals at once began sucking, and the artificial milk made them purr as it trickled slowly out.

"You'd better not let the captain find these things

116

on board," Heck warned. "He hates dogs. He'd probably shoot these critters."

"But they're so cute," Jerusha argued. She picked up one and hugged it, and the little fellow nibbled at her. "I'm going to tell the captain I can't dig anymore. Look at my hands," he said.

"You should have worn your gloves."

"They're too hot!"

Heck left his pups and stalked off.

He found the captain just waking up. Edge had been up all night and was in a bad humor. He listened to Heck's story and looked at his hands and said, "You should have worn gloves."

"They're too hot, and besides I didn't join the crew to dig. I'm a computer man."

"It won't hurt you to work a little bit, Heck."

Heck knew that the captain himself had put in several hours of pecking away at the hard, resistant soil.

Edge got up and went outside, listening with half an ear as Heck, following him, complained about the hard work. But when they got to where Ringo Smith was, the captain stopped and said, "What in the world is that thing?"

"It's an antigravity machine," Ringo said. "If it works, we won't have so much trouble walking. Look, it works like this." He showed the two observers the harness that one wore around his shoulders and waist. It looked like a small knapsack. Peering inside, Edge scowled at the mass of wires and said, "That's crazy. It'll never work."

"Sure it will. I'll be ready to try it pretty soon."

Edge looked disgusted. "If you don't have enough work to do on the ship, I can find some."

"Yes, you can take my place digging out there," Heck said. Still, he was fascinated, and when Edge left,

117

the two boys were arguing over some aspect of the invention.

Captain Edge made his tour of the ship, decided that all seemed well, then returned to his cabin. Opening the door, he stepped inside—and then stopped stock-still. "What in the name of—"

He looked around wildly, for although his cabin was not usually especially neat, now it was a total mess. His bedcover had been picked to pieces, and fuzzy fragments covered the floor. The door to his medicine chest was open, and every bottle was out, most of the contents emptied.

All at once a small movement caught his eye. He whirled, jerked back a pillow, and found a small, furry, striped animal chewing at the pillow and spitting out the pieces. With a roar Captain Edge hit his communicator. "Ensign Ericson, come to my cabin at once!"

Within moments, Jerusha appeared at the door. She stepped inside and took in the situation at once. "Oh, my! I've been looking for you." She scooped up the furry animal but stopped when Captain Edge barked at her.

"What is this—this *thing?* Is it yours?"

Jerusha said uncertainly, "Yes, sir. I'm afraid—"

"What is it?"

"Well, I don't know exactly, but it's so cute. Don't you think so?"

"I do *not* think it's cute, and look at the mess it's made out of my cabin!"

"Well, he just got away, sir. I was keeping them in the cargo hold, trying to raise them, and—"

"*Them!* There are more? I don't want to hear any of your excuses. Get this thing out of my cabin, then come back and clean up this mess!"

"Yes sir."

Edge stalked by her, shaking his head. "Making a menagerie out of my ship! You'll hear more from me about this, Ensign!"

Jerusha waited until the captain left, then slapped the furry pup on the bottom. "You naughty thing," she said. "Look what you've done. Come along. I'll put you back with your brothers and sisters."

Back in the cargo bay, she put him into the cage she had made, saying, "Now, no more trouble out of you."

Mei-Lani had been sitting there, poking her finger through the wire mesh. "They're so cute," she said.

"The captain doesn't think so. And you should see the mess that one made out of his cabin."

"What did he do?" Mei-Lani listened as Jerusha described the damage, then got up. "I'll help you clean it up, Jerusha."

The two girls went to Edge's cabin and began to create some order out of the mess. As they worked, Mei-Lani said, "I feel so helpless. The boys are out digging, but I can't do anything."

"You wouldn't be able to dig much, as tiny as you are," Jerusha said. "I tried it myself, and I didn't last fifteen minutes." She picked up the remains of the captain's blanket and stuffed it into a plastic bag. "I wish we were all as strong as Dai. I never saw anybody like him."

"What do you think will happen?"

"I think we're wasting our time. Something tells me that tridium is down deeper than we are able to dig with picks. We are going to have to do something to make peace with the Dulkins and get their help."

"They don't stop shooting at us long enough to listen. I wonder," Mei-Lani asked, giving a tentative look at Jerusha, "what the captain did to make them so mad?"

"I know what he did. He stole some tridium and betrayed their trust."

"That's the way it usually happens when explorers go into new cultures," Mei-Lani said. "I was reading last night about the Spanish who invaded the territory of the Indians in South America. They took all they had and killed off most of them."

"There's a lot of that kind of thing in history, isn't there?"

"I'm afraid so," Mei-Lani said. "I wish Captain Edge would see that he's got to win the confidence of the Dulkins somehow."

"There's a problem about that, though," Jerusha said. "If he goes to them, they could capture him. And once they get him, his body armor won't help him. They could cook him over a slow fire."

"I know it's dangerous, but, as he said, it may be the only way."

The two girls finished cleaning the captain's cabin, and when they left, they heard voices, loud voices.

"What is *that?*" Jerusha asked. She led the way down the corridor until they found Ringo and Heck pulling at some sort of device and arguing loudly.

"What are you two fighting about?" Mei-Lani asked.

Heck turned and said, "He's doing it all wrong. I'm trying to help him with our antigravity device."

Ringo stared at Heck, furious. "What do you mean, *our* device? This is my invention!"

"It'll never work unless you let me show you what's wrong with it."

"Yes, it will! I'm going outside and try it right now!"

"An antigravity device? That sounds interesting," Jerusha said. "How does it work?"

Ringo gave her a condescending look. "You wouldn't understand, Jerusha. It's too complicated."

Jerusha knew that Ringo was desperate to find some way to excel, so she merely shrugged. "Can I watch, then, as you try it?"

"Of course. Anybody can watch!" Ringo jerked the pack out of Heck's hand. "Except you, Heck!"

Heck said, "I can do what I want to! You're not my boss!"

"Well, watch, but keep your mouth shut!"

Ringo turned away and walked down the corridor. They all followed him through the portal.

At once the outside gravity pulled down at them, and Ringo complained, "It's like getting sucked into the earth. But wait until I get this done." He slipped the pack on his back, and Jerusha saw that he had a small control panel that fit over his chest. "Now watch this," he said. He began to manipulate the controls and soon cried, "It's working—it's working!"

Ringo began to straighten up. His face was bathed in smiles, and he waved his arms. "It's lifting me up. It's working!"

All three of them began to cheer—even Heck—but then they saw suddenly, with alarm, that Ringo was beginning to rise in the air.

"What are you doing, Ringo?" Mei-Lani cried.

But Ringo was too busy trying to manipulate the controls. He worked frantically, but slowly he continued rising until he was about twenty-five feet in the air, where he stopped.

"You'd better come down. You'll break your neck," Heck said.

"I can't. It won't work!"

Ringo felt like a fool. He saw others begin to come

121

out of the ship to see what the noise was about. Desperately he tried to reverse the controls. He was afraid that if he shut the device off completely, he would break his legs or his neck in the fall.

Tears of rage came to his eyes. *I can never do anything right,* he thought.

Then he saw Captain Edge come out. The captain said, "What are you doing up there, Smith?"

"Nothing, Captain."

"Well, come down at once."

"I can't, sir."

Down below there was consternation. He heard Edge mutter, "If he falls, he'll break his neck."

"I think I can get him down."

Studs Cagney whirled and disappeared into the ship. He came back quickly with a length of rope in his hand. Everyone watched as he made a noose, then began to swing it.

Mei-Lani said, "You look like a cowboy."

"What's a cowboy?" Raina asked curiously.

"Oh, they were in America a long time ago. They used what they called lassos to rope cattle. Ropes with nooses on the end, just like the one Studs has."

Cagney swung the loop expertly, threw it upward, and the noose caught Ringo's right foot. Studs pulled it tight and started tugging.

"Let me help." Dai joined him, and the two began to haul Ringo down.

"You're pulling my leg off!"

They ignored Ringo's screams.

Soon the boy was down, and Edge tripped the lock on the harness. Instantly the pack shot upward, and Ringo fell flat on his back.

The antigravity device sailed upward until it became a small dot and then disappeared.

"It's a good thing you got out of that," Captain Edge said grimly. "We'd have never gotten you down. You would have died in space."

Shakily Ringo got to his feet. "Well, I'm going to make another one. It almost worked!"

"We're never going to find the gems, Captain," Jerusha said. She stood beside the captain, who had been pacing the surface of Makon for nearly an hour. "You really ought not to be out here. The Dulkins might kidnap you."

Captain Edge glanced over to the ship, which made a light shadow against the darkness of the terrain. Makon's sun was going down now, sending orange streaks of light across the horizon. It was beautiful, in a way, but clearly Edge was in no mood to appreciate sunsets. He turned to Jerusha. "I don't know what else to do. I've been out trying to find the Dulkins, but when I do, they just keep shooting at me."

"You've got to regain their trust somehow, Captain. Mei-Lani and I have been talking about it. You've broken faith with them, and, therefore, you've got to prove that you can be honest."

"How do I do that?" Edge growled.

Jerusha came closer, studying his face. It was a handsome face, though she would never admit that to him. He was also a stubborn man and capable of rather devious behavior. She said, "First of all, you have to *be* honest."

"What's that supposed to mean?" Edge demanded. "I *am* honest."

"No, you're not, Captain," Jerusha said deliberately. "You stole from these people and betrayed them. Why shouldn't they shoot at us? You taught them that we're dishonest and that we're out to hurt them."

"I only took a few little samples, and I lost them," he complained.

"I think you're going to have to do more than you've been doing."

"What are you talking about? I'm the captain here!"

Jerusha studied Edge carefully. "What makes you so hard, Captain Edge?"

He looked at her. "Hard? I'm not hard."

"Yes, you are. On the outside, at least." Jerusha had always felt that there was another side to him in addition to the side that could steal and practice dishonesty. "What was your childhood like?"

"I didn't have any childhood."

"Of course, you did. Everybody has a childhood."

Edge seemed to be studying the hard crust of the planet. "I never knew my parents. They died in an accident in space six months after I was born."

"Oh, I'm so sorry!" This shed new light on the captain. "Who did you grow up with?"

"Different relatives. I was shifted around from place to place. I never had a home. I finally got with an uncle who intended to work me to death—or beat me to death. So when I got big enough, I did the beating and walked out."

Jerusha said, "It must've been very hard." Her voice was soft, not sharp and clipped as it usually was.

Edge looked up quickly. "It was hard enough," he said, "but I survived. I learned to engineer a little, took some interstellar flights, and found out I could be as good a pilot as any after a while."

"Why didn't you go to the Space Academy?"

Suddenly he grinned. "I did. Didn't you know that?"

"Why, no."

"I got kicked out just as you did. Probably for about the same reasons—being a rebel."

This made Jerusha feel very close, indeed, to the captain. "I didn't know that, sir."

"Well, you know it now." Edge said no more for a time but stood staring out into the fast-growing darkness. "Have you ever been married?"

"No."

Edge's answer was so short that Jerusha was stunned. He seemed angry. "Why are you so angry? All I asked was if you'd ever had a wife."

"And I told you no!"

"Well, you must've had a sweetheart or two."

Capt. Mark Edge turned to her. "I had one once," he said grimly. "She told me she loved me more than anything on earth—and then she ran away with my best friend."

Jerusha said nothing, but she sensed again the grief and the hurt that lay deep in this tough-looking man. "I'm very sorry, Mark," she said, unaware that she was using his first name.

Edge looked at her. The darkness was almost complete now, and he had to lean forward. "Well, it's happened to better men than me. I don't cry over it."

"It might be better if you did."

"Cry? Me?"

"What's wrong with that?"

"Men don't cry. Women do that."

"Not always. One of the bravest men I ever knew cried. I saw him. He wasn't afraid of anything in the world."

"Well, I'm not a crybaby."

Jerusha thought, *He'd be better off if he would cry. He bottles up all his anger and grief and won't let it get out—but he'll never believe that.* Aloud she said, "I'm sorry if I insulted you, Captain, about your honesty. But it's true enough, you know."

Edge stood there. "Maybe you're right, but it's too late to do anything about me now. I can't change what I am."

"But you can be changed." She hesitated, then said, "Some of us are Christians. We've all been changed."

Edge shifted uncomfortably. "I'm not religious."

Jerusha saw that he was adamant and would not listen, so she said finally, "Someday you may want to talk about it. When you do, then you might talk to me or Raina."

Edge did not answer. She suspected that religious talk made him nervous.

He said, "We'd better get back to the ship."

11

A Loving God

As the days went on, life on Makon became more difficult. Every day's activity was practically the same as the day before—the strongest members going out and trying to find samples of tridium. No one was allowed to wander far from the ship for fear of the Dulkins, and monotony began to set in.

Bronwen Llewellen organized a Christian service in the largest area of the ship, the mess hall, which was shared by all for recreation and dining. It was a relatively large space where all the crew could meet at one time. But not everyone was sympathetic. Tara Jaleel protested to the captain, saying, "What about those of us who don't want any religion? Don't we have any rights?"

"Lieutenant, you have plenty of time to do whatever you please in the mess hall."

Edge himself did not attend the services, at least not openly. He did come in once while the service was going on, ostensibly to get something to drink from the galley. As he entered, he saw that Raina was standing up while others were seated. She was wearing a simple two-piece garment of light green, and her auburn hair glowed against it. She had in her hands what he supposed was a Bible and was reading from it. He drew himself a drink of pear cider and listened.

"Our God does not condemn people. As it says in the Bible in the book of John, chapter three, verse sixteen, 'For God so loved the world, that He gave His only begotten Son, that whoever believes in Him shall not perish, but have eternal life.'"

After she finished reading, Raina began to say in her quiet voice, "This is a large galaxy. There are thousands of worlds, and on many worlds there are people, human colonists. Some are like our chief engineer, Ivan Petroski, from the planet Bellinka. All the people on his world are small. On the planet Mentor, the humans are albinos and live deep underground. The people who colonized the planet Carmine all have black eyes and reddish skin. The Dulkins on this planet are short, stout, and exceptionally strong. All these people are different in many ways, physically, and emotionally, and mentally, but they have one thing in common . . ."

Raina looked around at her small audience, then lifted her eyes to meet the gaze of Captain Edge. "They all are lost." She saw Edge's eyes flicker and his head shake, but went on. "It's been many hundreds of years since space travel and the colonization of all these planets began. The inhabitants of the original Earth are now all over the galaxy. But they are not aliens—they are all humans, and all sprang from Adam and Eve. And since they did, that means they all share the heritage of sin."

Studs Cagney, strangely enough, had chosen to attend several of the services. He always sat with his back to the wall, his eyes fixed on the girl, listening with a cynical air. Nevertheless he kept coming, and today, as Raina began to speak of Jesus, he leaned forward with interest.

"God is two things: He is loving, and He is just," Raina said. Her light green eyes were alive with excitement. "God made all of us to have fellowship with Him, but when the first man sinned, that fellowship was broken. Now man had no God, or he had a God that was angry with his sin. What could he do? He could bring animal sacrifices, but the Bible says that would never do away with sin."

She talked about how animal sacrifices really were only a kind of picture of something that was to come. Then she said, "But one day John the Baptist looked up and saw a man, and he cried out, 'Behold, the Lamb of God who takes away the sin of the world!'

"At last," Raina said, "the reality had come. Jesus was the sacrifice that God Himself had planned, and when Jesus died on the cross, almost the last thing He said was, 'It is finished.' He meant that now there was a way that all of us who are lost can be found again by trusting in the Lamb of God."

And Studs Cagney listened with disbelief but also with something like hope in his face.

Raina smiled at him, then her eyes went to Captain Edge, but Edge's eyes were hooded, and he abruptly turned and left the mess hall.

After the service Raina and Jerusha spoke of what had happened. "Did you see Captain Edge leave when I was talking about Jesus?" Raina asked.

"Yes. He has a hard side to him, doesn't he?"

"He does. But somehow, when people hear of Jesus, it does something to them. I don't know what it is or how it works, but I know how it was for me. I didn't want any religion at all until I heard a sermon about Jesus and His blood and how He could make me free."

Jerusha nodded. "There is power in the name of Jesus," she agreed. "The captain's a hard man because he's had a hard life, Raina."

"I suppose so, but he needs Christ just like everyone else. I pray for him every day."

Jerusha nodded. "I think you should. All of us should."

The two girls suddenly were alerted by the sound of gunfire exploding outside the ship. They ran to a porthole and looked out.

"It's just the Dulkins attacking again."

"I wish we had some way just to talk to them!" Raina exclaimed.

Inside the control room, Tara Jaleel exclaimed, "Captain, we've got to do something! Why don't we make an attack on them? Then we can capture their leaders and make them listen to us!"

She knew Edge was highly tempted. Nothing else had worked. He had gone out alone several times but—aside from being shot at—had accomplished nothing.

"No, we can't do that," he said finally. "We have to find a peaceful solution."

This did not satisfy Lieutenant Jaleel, but there was nothing she could say to change his mind. "We may as well go home," she said. "We will never make those people listen!"

The day after the service, Ringo left his station and went outside. He saw Raina in the distance and walked toward her. As he did, he thought, *She's the prettiest girl I ever saw, but I might as well be a piece of stone for all the attention she ever pays to me.*

"Hello, Raina."

"Oh, hello, Ringo!" Raina turned and looked back at the ship. "Is there anything wrong?"

"No, I just wanted—" Ringo wanted to say, "I just wanted to be with you, Raina," but he could not force himself to say it. Instead, he said, "I just wanted to go for a walk." He waited for her to invite him to join her, and when she did, his face lit up. The two walked for about half an hour, talking about the situation. It was hard walking in the heavy gravity, but just being close to Raina made Ringo feel lighter.

"I enjoyed the service yesterday, Raina," he said finally.

"Did you, Ringo? I'm glad." She smiled at him, and there was a prettiness in her face that he suspected she herself did not know.

The two walked on across the broken ground. Raina asked him about the new invention he was working on, and he spoke of it eagerly.

They were far from the *Daystar* when, suddenly, three shadowy figures leaped from behind rocks and began running toward them.

"Raina! It's the Dulkins! Run for the ship!"

Ringo fled in panic. When he dared, he looked back and saw Raina scrambling to her feet. She had obviously stumbled and fallen flat. But the Dulkins were almost on her, and neither of them had worn their body armor!

Fear rose in him. He wanted to run to her, but as the dark squatty figures, crying with excitement, surrounded her, he was afraid.

As Ringo stood there trying to make himself go forward, a figure shot by him. It was Dai Bando.

Dai ran straight toward Raina, where she was struggling with the three natives. He hit them as a bowling ball hits pins and scattered them. But they instantly leaped up and began battering Dai with the long staffs that they wielded. They appeared not to be carrying guns, but the heavy staffs could crush a man's skull instantly.

Dai Bando ducked under one, then reached out and grabbed the wrist of the Dulkin, who was shorter than he but muscular and strong. With a single flip, Dai twisted the arm and sent the man hurtling through the air. He landed on his back and did not get up, seemingly so stunned that he could not move.

Raina was on her feet but was helpless to assist Dai. She stood watching the wicked-looking staffs swish through the air. Each time, Dai allowed the staff to pass over his head, and she marveled at his reflexes.

Finally Dai reached out and plucked the staff from the hand of one of the Dulkins. He reversed it, shoved the end into the burly native's stomach, and drove the wind out of him. Instantly he whirled and caught the staff that was coming down on his own head with the one he held in his hands. He jerked the weapon from the angry native and then sent a whistling blow that deliberately missed the man's head.

The Dulkin stumbled back with a cry of alarm. The other two were now getting up, but they had had enough. Whirling, they ran off and disappeared. Accustomed to the gravity, they moved as quickly as running wolves.

"Are you all right, Raina?"

"Yes." She put out her hand, and when Dai took it, she smiled at him. "If you hadn't come, they would have had me."

"I'm glad I was here then," Dai said. "Come. Let's get back to the *Daystar.*"

When they came to where Ringo was standing, Raina saw that his face was white.

"It's OK," Dai said cheerfully. "No problem."

Ringo turned without a word and trudged off.

"What's the matter with him?" Dai asked in surprise, looking at Raina.

But she understood at once. "At this moment he hates himself and he hates you and he hates me, Dai. He's embarrassed that he didn't come to my help."

"It's a good thing he didn't," Dai said. "They would have captured both of you. He's no match for three of those fellows."

Raina did not answer. She knew how bad Ringo felt and determined to make it up to him.

When they got back to the ship, she went to him at once. "Well, that was pretty bad, but it turned out all right."

"No thanks to me," Ringo said. He turned his head away.

He did not fool Raina, however. There had been tears of frustration and humiliation in his eyes. She put her hands on his shoulders. "We all have different talents, Ringo. If our lives depended on the computer, Dai couldn't help us at all. It just happened that he had the talent for this particular crisis."

Clearly, her words did not help Ringo. He was humiliated beyond words, and he pulled away from her without answering.

Later, Raina related the incident to Jerusha. "Ringo feels bad about it. He thinks he could have done something."

"He admires you a lot, and he hated to be shown up in front of you."

"Does he? Well, he's a nice guy, and I like him."

"He won't like Dai after this. No one likes to be shown up."

It was only half an hour later that a cry of alarm went through the *Daystar*. Heck and Ivan Petroski had been arguing over some scientific element of the ship, when the dwarf suddenly stopped shouting and said, "What's that?"

The two turned to see that one of the grunts had come on board, a tall, strong-looking fellow named Myron. His face visor was shattered.

"The Dulkins got them!" Myron gasped.

"Who? What happened?" Petroski demanded.

"It's the first officer and that little girl, Mei-Lani. The Dulkins got 'em!"

The alarm went out, and soon the entire crew was gathered, listening as white-faced Myron told his story.

"We'd gotten out a little bit far from the ship, and they jumped us. They weren't shooting, but they caught us by surprise. They were just carrying big sticks. That's what broke my face mask. Then they grabbed the first officer and the girl. I fought 'em off and broke two of their heads with my staff, but they got the other two."

Capt. Mark Edge had a harsh light in his eyes. "Well, it's what I feared."

"What will happen now, Captain?" Jerusha asked, thinking of the tender young Mei-Lani in the hands of the brutish Dulkins. She felt responsible. After all, it had been she who had asked Mei-Lani to come on this voyage.

"We'll have to wait and see," Edge said. "I think they'll use them for blackmail—threaten to kill them if we don't do what they want."

Jerusha stared at the hard face of the captain and saw the bleakness in his gray eyes. She did not ask what he would do, but she was afraid for her friend and for the first officer.

12

Chief Locar

Ivan Petroski and Tara Jaleel met with the captain to discuss strategy.

"We must attack at once!" Jaleel demanded. Her eyes gleamed with a fierce light, and her body was tense.

"No, Captain, that would never do!" Petroski countered. "In the first place, have you ever thought what would happen if *you* got killed? The rest of us would be stranded here."

"I can pilot this ship!" Jaleel exclaimed.

"And what if something happens to the navigator? We'd wander for a thousand years without finding our way out."

Jaleel had no answer to that, but her instinct always was to attack. She said, "I still say we're responsible for our companions. We must rescue them."

"We don't even know where they are," Mark Edge said wearily. "We've had no message from the Dulkins." He passed his hand over his eyes and tried to think. The kidnapping of the girl disturbed him greatly. He had grown fond of Mei-Lani. He had spent several evenings in her company, listening to her talk knowledgeably of ancient poets and philosophers. She was so tiny, so helpless! "We've got to do something," he said in desperation, "but I don't yet know what!"

The discussion went on for some time until, suddenly, the meeting was interrupted. Jerusha came to the door, her eyes alert. "Captain, we have a message!" She held up what looked like a stone wrapped in paper.

"Where did you get that?" Edge demanded.

"A guard saw one of the Dulkins approaching. He didn't get very close, but he threw this stone. I think this is a message wrapped around it."

Eagerly Captain Edge unwrapped the paper and put down the stone. He smoothed out the message. "I can't read this! It's in Dulkinese!"

"On the back!" Jerusha said. "That's Mei-Lani's writing on the back!"

Captain Edge read out loud. "Captain Edge, First Officer Thrax and I have not been harmed. However, the leader of the Dulkins instructs me to tell you that if you do not surrender the ship and our people, the first officer and I will be killed. First Officer Thrax and I ask you to do what is best for the *ship*, not for us."

"Well, that ties it!" the captain said, throwing the paper down on the table. "What are we supposed to do now?"

"We'll have to do what they demand," Jerusha said quietly.

"Surrender? Never!" This, of course, came from the warlike Tara Jaleel, who drew herself up to her full six feet. "I have never surrendered, and I never will! Thrax and Mei-Lani knew what they were getting into when they signed on for this trip!"

Ivan Petroski, the shortest person present, drew himself up to his full height and glared at Jaleel. "Do you think I'd be responsible for the death of Zeno and that young girl? Maybe you have no concept of sacrifice, but I do! On the planet of Bellinka, not a soul there would consider sacrificing two companions to save himself."

The argument raged hot and furious between the dwarf and the tall Tara Jaleel.

Finally, Edge held a hand up. "It's not an easy decision," he said. "If it were just me, I wouldn't hesitate. But the crew didn't sign on to be sacrificed. Who knows? They might kill us all and then the first officer and Mei-Lani as well. I'll have to think about it."

"Think quickly, Captain," Jerusha said. "We don't know these people. You know them better than most. Are they cruel?"

"They are not a gentle people," Edge admitted, a worried look on his face. He knew Jerusha was right, but his mind was spinning. "Leave me alone! I must think! We'll have another meeting in an hour."

"This is not totally unlike my home." Zeno Thrax looked around, and there was almost a peaceful expression on his face.

Mei-Lani's eyes were still unaccustomed to the semidarkness, and she squinted. One small candle was burning. She saw that they were in a room carved out of stone. The flame flickered, and the pale features of Zeno became clearer. "Your home is like this?"

"Yes. As I told you, we all live underground. The surface of our planet is too hot to bear. I suppose that's why we've lost all of our coloration," he said quietly. Sitting on one of the crude benches, he appeared to be relaxed. He studied her face. "Are you afraid, Mei-Lani?"

"No. I was a little frightened when they first captured us, but if they were going to kill us they would have already done it."

"I wouldn't be too sure of that," Zeno warned. "They may want to have a public execution. But I suspect," he added, "they're going to use us for hostages."

"That would be logical." Mei-Lani nodded. She sat back, her shoulders resting against the rough stones. "If Jerusha were here, she could probably sense something about what these people are feeling. They're so rough-looking, I can't tell a thing."

Indeed, the Dulkins of Makon were a rough-looking race. The small party that had seized Mei-Lani and Zeno was squatty and thickset. Their long dark hair fell over their faces. Their features were blunt and cruel. Still, they had not harmed the two captives.

"I've been on many planets and seen many races," Zeno said quietly. "Most of them, after you get to know them, are pretty much alike. After all," he said, "we're all human, even though we look different and some of us behave very badly."

"That's right, Zeno," Mei-Lani said. "There was a man named C. S. Lewis, who lived back in England in the days before space travel. He was opposed to space travel. He said everywhere man goes, he pollutes, and if man expanded throughout the universe, not just Earth, then every planet would be polluted."

"He must've been a wise man. That's pretty much what has happened." He looked at the girl and said, "You've studied so much history. Do you know of any case where humans ever went to a new world and made it better?"

Sorrowfully Mei-Lani shook her head. Her black hair had come loose from its ribbon and fell over her eyes. She pushed it back and patted it, then said, "No, not as a whole. It's the news of Jesus that makes things better for all who trust in Him. If Captain Edge would only listen to Jerusha—"

"And to you," Zeno said. "I know you've tried to get him to take a softer approach to the Dulkins."

"It's the only thing that will work. Jesus is the Prince of Peace."

Thrax fell silent for a while, and before he could speak again, the door swung open. Three men came in, all wearing the crude fur capes that the Dulkins wore. One of them was larger than the others and obviously had some sort of authority. He said, "So these are the captives. They look weak."

"We're all weak, sir," Mei-Lani said, "but we trust in your hospitality."

Shock was reflected in the dark eyes of the tallest man. "You speak our language," he said. "How is that?"

Mei-Lani knew many languages and had studied the general language groups that existed in the part of the galaxy where they were headed. The dialect and diction of the leader of the Dulkins were somewhat different, but still she could understand him.

"I have studied your language, sir," she said. "My name is Mei-Lani Lao, and this is the first officer of the *Daystar*, Zeno Thrax."

For a moment the leader stood puzzled. Clearly, he had not expected anything like this. At last he said, "I am Chief Locor."

"We are happy to make your acquaintance, Chief Locor." Mei-Lani rose and bowed low, and Zeno Thrax, seeing her do this, imitated her action. "We come in peace."

Locor snarled. "I know your peace. I have watched your people. Your captain is the same one who was here some time ago. He robbed us and betrayed us."

"That may be so," Mei-Lani said, "but he wants now to come in peace."

"I do not believe you! You are spies, and you've come to take our lands and our gems!"

139

"No, Chief, that is not the truth. It's like this . . ." Mei-Lani said.

She began to speak, and the chief listened, drawn up to his full height. When she had finished making her plea, without a word he turned and stepped out of the prison cell, followed by the other two. The door slammed.

Zeno said, "Well, I hope you have another plan. I couldn't understand what he said, but he obviously doesn't trust us."

"There's no reason why they should. Trust is only built when there's honor," Mei-Lani said.

Time passed slowly. Perhaps an hour later, two guards came into the cell, one with a heavy sword in his hand, the other carrying a bowl of food. Without a word he put the bowl on the table.

Mei-Lani said, "Thank you," in the Dulkin language.

He stared at her in consternation, then said, "Yes," and turned and left the room.

They stood, looking down at the food.

"What do you suppose it is?" Zeno said. "We'd better eat, but it smells terrible."

"It may taste worse, but we've *got* to eat. We don't know how long we'll be here, or when we'll be fed again. Do you mind if I ask a blessing?"

Zeno peered at her. "Go ahead."

"Lord, we thank You for this food and for taking care of us and for our companions back on the ship. In Jesus' name."

Mei-Lani took a morsel from the bowl. It appeared to be some kind of meat. Her eyes opened wide and then shut tight.

"Is it that bad?" Zeno said. He picked up a chunk of the meat and tasted it, and his shoulders quivered. "It's probably lizard, or maybe worm."

"Zeno, don't talk like that! Just eat it!"

The two ate as much as they could, then drank some of the water that was in a stone jug. At least it was sweet tasting. "The water's good," she said cheerfully.

"Yes." Zeno sat on a bench. "Now, we've got a lot of time to spend together. You've read many books, and I know very little. Tell me about some of the books you've read."

Both Zeno and Mei-Lani were resting when the door opened again with a loud noise. They sat up immediately. Three guards stood there, all with heavy swords.

"Come," one said.

"Where are you taking us?" Mei-Lani asked as they were led out of the cell and down a twisting corridor carved out of stone. At intervals, torches set in iron holders gave forth a flickering light.

"To the tribal council," a guard answered. Then he said, "You are not Dulkin. How do you speak our tongue?"

"I learned it out of a book."

"A book? What is a book?"

"It's—well, I don't know how to explain it," Mei-Lani said. "They're very primitive," she said to Zeno, "but I don't feel that they're *evil*."

"No, they're very much like my own people. I guess living underground does something to you."

They were taken to a cavernous room where seven men sat behind a stone table. Locor, the chief, waited until the guards backed away. Then he said, "Now, the council wants to know what you are doing on our planet."

141

"I cannot speak for the captain," Mei-Lani said carefully. "I understand that he has a mission here, and he wants very much to talk with you, Chief Locor. He has gone out many times trying to find you, but always your people shot at him, or ran from him, or tried to attack him."

"Why should we not? Did he not betray us?"

"I think he regrets that." Still more carefully, Mei-Lani did the best she could to quietly explain how things had changed.

There was silence from the seven. Their faces seemed as hard and cold as the stone that surrounded them.

"You are but a child. I cannot talk with you," the chief said at last.

"None of the others speak your language. That is my responsibility—to learn the languages of different peoples and to interpret for the captain."

"Who is this white one? I never saw one so white."

"His name is Zeno Thrax, and he comes from a planet much like your own. As a matter of fact, he says he feels great kinship with you. He feels that all people who live under the surface are alike in some ways."

The chief stared at Zeno and said, "Are you an honorable man?"

Zeno bowed. "I hope my word may be trusted. I have never broken it. My people punish lying severely—by execution."

Chief Locor studied the white face of the Mentoran. He seemed to find something there that he could trust, for he said, "This captain of yours. *He* is not a man of honor and truth."

When Mei-Lani interpreted, Zeno did not hesitate. "He is basically a good man, sir, but he has made a severe error in dealing with your people. He knows

142

that now. I think if you would see him, you would find that he is willing to admit his wrong."

After Mei-Lani translated Zeno's words, there was a furious debate among the council members.

Zeno leaned toward her and whispered, "What are they arguing about?"

"Some of them do not want to trust Captain Edge. They want him to leave and never come back. Others seemed willing to try a peace party."

Finally Chief Locor held up his hand, and the muttering stopped. He looked at the two prisoners. "We have not been fortunate with out-worlders visiting our planet. Many come to enslave us and abuse us. One ship came and hunted our people simply for sport. They cut off heads and used them for trophies. We do not trust any people but our own."

"I can understand how you might feel that way, Chief Locor," Mei-Lani said. "But you have us as your hostages. Will you not meet with the captain on your own terms? You may keep us here and meet with him in a different place, if you like. You can always execute us if you cannot arrange terms with the captain."

Locor said, "You are unusual—a frail girl and not afraid to die."

"I serve a God who is Lord of life, and after death I will be closer to Him."

Locor gaped at her. "How can He help you if you are dead?"

"He, too, was dead once, but He came back from the dead. And now, those who die believing in Him— He takes them to Himself."

"What is your God's name?"

"His name is Jesus Christ."

The councilmen were listening intently, and Locor said, "I would hear more of this. If you are not executed, perhaps I will allow you to speak to me and to the council so that we can hear more of this Jesus Christ."

"Thank you, Chief. I would count it an honor to do so."

Locor turned to the man on his right. "Let the girl prepare a message for the captain. Tell him that I will meet with him. And that the meeting will determine whether these two live or die."

When they were again in their prison, Zeno said, "What do you think will happen, Mei-Lani?"

"I don't know, but it's in God's hands."

"In God's hands," Zeno mused. He thought about that for a while. "It might be very pleasant, indeed, to have one's life in God's hands—if God were good. Some gods are evil and harsh."

"Jesus is good. He is the God of love."

Zeno Thrax sat quietly on his bunk, his arms around his knees, his legs drawn up. "That sounds very wonderful," he muttered. "A God of love . . ."

13
A Kiss from Captain Edge

Everyone was staring at Captain Edge in a suspenseful manner. Ringo thought even the room itself felt tense. Half an hour ago, a Dulkin had walked boldly up to the spaceship and handed a message to Ivan Petroski, and he quickly brought it to the captain. At once, the captain had called a meeting.

Bronwen Llewellen and Tara Jaleel sat on opposite sides of the table, looking like opposite mirror images. Tara Jaleel was fierce and warlike in appearance; the older woman was gentle and had no anger for anyone.

Ringo and Heck sat side by side. Raina and Dai Bando were across from them. Ringo was watching Raina furtively and still thinking of how he had turned coward and refused to go to her aid. He had gone over the scene a thousand times and could not excuse himself for it. Although Raina had told him more than once that it was not important, to Ringo it had become very important indeed.

"I'll read this aloud," Captain Edge said. "It's from Mei-Lani again, addressed to me, and it says, 'We have been able to work out a meeting with Chief Locor. He is really more than a local chief. He is more like a king of the scattered tribes on Makon. His terms are simple. You are to come unarmed away from the ship, without body armor, and surrender yourself to a party that the chief will send. I strongly urge you to do this, Captain Edge, for I feel that these are basically people of good will who have been badly used in the past. I believe that if you can talk face-to-face with them, the differences can be all taken care of.'"

Lifting his head, Captain Edge stared around the room. He started to speak, but before he could say a word, Tara Jaleel said, "Don't do it, Captain. It's a trap! Once they have you, we'll have difficulty getting the ship off the planet. And we don't have enough people for a rescue party."

"I think we'll have to chance that, Lieutenant Jaleel." The captain spoke slowly, and Ringo saw no sign of fear in him. Perhaps, as a matter of fact, he felt great relief, for here at last was something he could do. He really had no other choice if he wanted to save the lives of his executive officer and the girl. "I'll go at once," he announced.

"Who'll be in charge while you're gone, Captain?" Tara Jaleel asked.

"In the absence of the first officer, you will be, Tara. I trust you implicitly. If it doesn't go well with us," he said slowly and with great emphasis, "there will be no rescue attempts. Get the ship off as quickly as you can. Mrs. Llewellen will navigate you back to earth."

Bronwen Llewellen suddenly smiled. She said something in a foreign language, but Edge did not ask her to translate.

As Captain Edge prepared to step outside the spaceship, Dai Bando said, "Did you understand what my aunt said to you?"

"No. What was it?"

"An ancient Welsh saying. She's repeated it to me often." The dark-haired boy smiled. "She said it would go well with you, for the hand of our God is upon you."

The words caused the captain to start. "Well, I've never had anything like *that* said about me. I'm not a man of God, you know, Dai."

"Nevertheless, that's what she said. I wish you'd take me with you, Captain."

"No. I want you here." He turned to the boy and said, "I was against bringing you on this trip, Dai, but you've been a great help. I don't know what we would have done without Studs Cagney, and you seem to have tamed him."

Dai Bando felt embarrassed. "He's really a decent man underneath all that toughness."

"I think you may be right. In any case, let's shake hands. If I don't make it back, I want you to know you've been good for the *Daystar.*"

They clasped hands, and then Dai Bando watched the captain walk rapidly away, not turning to look back. "He's a decent man himself," Dai muttered, "but he doesn't know it." He watched until Mark Edge disappeared.

As soon as the *Daystar* was out of sight, the captain expected the party of Dulkins to step out at any moment and capture him. Then he heard a sound just behind him. He whirled and cried involuntarily, "Jerusha!"

"Hello, Captain." Jerusha came up quickly and stood waiting for him to speak.

"What are *you* doing here?"

"I thought you might need help to know what the Dulkins are like."

"You weren't at the meeting."

"I heard what happened, though. I knew if I asked you to let me come you'd say no, so I didn't give you the chance to turn me down." She smiled fetchingly.

"Please don't be angry, Captain. I mean, after all, we're in this together, aren't we?"

The anger and impatience that had risen in Mark Edge seemed to fade away. *This girl always knows exactly what's going on.* "Well," he muttered, "you're here. I might as well let you come."

"Thank you, Captain."

Edge and Jerusha had walked not more than two hundred yards when a voice suddenly spoke behind them. They turned quickly to see a band of warriors armed with odd rifles in their hands. The leader said something in Dulkin, then waved them forward.

"I think he means for us to go ahead of them," Edge said.

They walked on, the warriors following. Edge asked, "So, what do you think of these people?"

"They're rough and rather primitive. That's certain from their appearance," Jerusha said. "But they don't seem vicious. I think they're more *curious* about us than anything else."

Indeed, the band of Dulkins was now crowded closely about them, staring, putting them in a sort of living cell as they walked along, but making no attempt to harm them.

Finally, the leader waved Jerusha and the captain toward an opening in a sheer bluff.

"I think this is their door. The door to their underground dwelling," Jerusha said. "I never did like tight places, especially underground. I went into a cave once. It had all kinds of beautiful crystals in it, but I was terrified the whole time."

"Well, I'm glad to hear you're afraid of something." Mark smiled. "Come on. Give me your hand."

Willingly Jerusha took his hand, for she *was* afraid. She was not afraid of many things, but somehow, when

148

she was underground, she felt that she was being buried alive. However, the captain's hand was strong, and as they moved down a gloomy corridor lit by torches set in the side walls, she whispered, "I'm glad I've got you here, Mark. I'd be frightened to death if I were alone."

"We'll be all right."

They walked a long way, making several turns. The tunnel widened, and the torches became more abundant. And then they came to a door guarded by four armed men.

"I've got the feeling this is it. Say your prayers."

Jerusha looked at him quickly. "I am."

Mark Edge looked somewhat embarrassed. "I didn't mean that literally."

"I did," Jerusha said. "It's always good to pray. And not only when we need something, but just because it's good to talk to God. You'll find out someday, Captain Edge."

The door swung open, and Jerusha and Captain Edge stepped inside. There, behind a long stone table, sat seven men. Edge's name was called, and he wheeled to see Mei-Lani and Zeno Thrax back in the shadows. At once he stepped over and shook the hand of his first officer. "Are you all right, Zeno?"

"Why, yes, Captain. Things have been very pleasant."

Jerusha threw her arms around Mei-Lani and hugged her. "I've been so worried about you, Mei-Lani."

Mei-Lani patted the tall girl on the shoulder. "It's all right. You'll see." Then she turned to the captain. "I'll have to be your interpreter, Captain."

"It's incredible that you speak their language!" Jerusha said excitedly.

"I brushed up some on the trip out. I had a feeling someone would need to speak to these people."

"Well, bless you!"

All four of them turned to the council then, and Mei-Lani said in the Dulkin language, "Chief Locor, this is Captain Mark Edge, the commander of the *Daystar*. And this is Ensign Jerusha Ericson, one of the officers."

Locor looked at the girl for a moment, but his main attention was put on Mark Edge. "We meet again," he said.

Mei-Lani interpreted this, and Mark flushed. "Tell him I'm truly sorry for the way I behaved on my last mission here. It was very wrong and not at all the act of a good man or a gentleman. I am very sorry and ask the chief's pardon."

While Mei-Lani was translating this, Jerusha was staring hard at the chief's face. "I can't make him out," she whispered to Zeno. "What do you think?"

"I think he's very angry, but he's waiting to see what the captain does."

Locor listened until Mei-Lani had finished interpreting. Then he said, "By our law you deserve death, Captain Edge."

"That is up to you and the council," Edge said evenly. "While I'm in this place, I'm under your law."

A murmur went up from the council as Mei-Lani translated, and Jerusha felt some sort of approval in their response.

But Locor remained silent, and they all waited. These were primitive people, and it would not be impossible that he would use his absolute powers to execute Edge. Jerusha felt herself tensing up and willing the chief to say that he was ready to forgive.

The silence ran on for a long time, but finally Chief Locor nodded briefly. "We will accept your apology."

"Thank you, Chief. I'm sincerely sorry and trust that in the future you will find me an honest and honorable man."

"Since I'm not going to execute you," Chief Locor said—and a flicker of humor touched his dark eyes— "we will now have a meal together."

The meal turned into a banquet.

Mei-Lani whispered some of the Dulkin customs to the captain as they ate. "They only break bread with people that they accept, so the fact that they're eating with you proves that you don't have to worry anymore, Captain Edge."

"Well, that's good news," Edge said with relief.

"I know they look pretty bad, rough and all of that," Mei-Lani said, "but they are really a very wonderful people."

"They are very different from us in appearance, at least," Edge said.

"But appearances don't really matter, do they? What does matter is the heart. They have receptive hearts."

"What do you mean, 'receptive hearts'?"

"I mean I've been telling some of them about the God who forgives, about Jesus and the Father. They were very open. Already two of the guards have accepted Jesus as their God."

Edge stared at her in amazement, then his eyes lifted to Jerusha, who was listening with a smile. "Is she always like this, Jerusha?"

"Always, Captain. She's the finest evangelist I've ever seen. Except, perhaps, for Raina."

Edge shook his head. "Well, I'll believe anything now."

"Not all of these people know how to read and

write, but they have wonderfully retentive memories. Their history goes back for thousands of years, and they have it all in legend and song. I expect we'll hear some of those stories. Did you ever hear of the Vikings?"

"It seems I have somewhere. Weren't they sailors who conquered parts of the world in their little ships?"

"Yes, and they had bards at their banquets who would recite the stories of famous battles. One of the stories was about a warrior called Beowulf. It's a wonderful story. There was a very brave man who faced a monster. I expect we'll hear something like that after the meal."

They did not have to wait until after the meal, for an old man came in and in a strong, steady voice began to chant. Mei-Lani translated his story, and it was about an ancient king who risked his life and finally gave his life for his people.

"They honor those who give their lives for their people, and they would die for their nation at any time. The good Dulkins, that is."

"That is a good story. Tell the chief I liked it very much and wish I could be more like the hero."

The chief looked pleased.

After a huge meal of unpleasant-tasting food, the chief said, "We will now talk about our future. There will be no argument, Captain Edge. You want the gems that my people mine. And we want to learn how to improve our condition. We have been told about what you call 'books.' This Mei-Lani has told us that books are a way for us to enjoy our songs even when the bard is not here."

"Why, we can help you with all of that!" Captain Edge exclaimed.

Locor held up his hands. "Then this is what we will

do. No one except you or your agent may come here. We Dulkins will do the mining. You will bring us tools and the other things we need."

When Mei-Lani translated this, the first officer nodded. "Take it, Captain. It's a good deal," Zeno Thrax said out of the side of his mouth.

Mei-Lani added her words. "I think the first officer is right."

"It isn't bad, Captain Edge," Jerusha said. "It really means that you'll have a monopoly on tridium."

"I never thought of that," Edge said. His mind began to work, but he was jolted when Jerusha said, "We can see to it that the price paid for the tridium is more than fair. These people need our help, don't they, Captain?"

"Well—" Edge cleared his throat "—I suppose they do. Very well. What do we do? Shake hands on it?"

"No, you have to kiss the cheek of the chief." As Mei-Lani said this, a mischievous smile curled up the corners of her mouth. "I assure you, it's the custom here. When the king makes an agreement, it is only valid if the person he agrees with gives him a ceremonial kiss."

Zeno Thrax was laughing silently. Mark gave him a furious look. "Shut up, First!" Then he turned to Jerusha, who was also covering a smile with her hand. "Ensign," he said, "*you* go give him a kiss."

"No, it has to be you," Mei-Lani said. "Quick, they are waiting!"

Mark Edge had faced dangerous moments. He had risked his life more than once. But he could not think of a time that was any harder for him. Swallowing again, he advanced, bowed, then leaned forward and kissed the dark cheek of the chieftain.

Locor immediately seized his shoulders and

kissed him roughly on the forehead. "Now," he said, "we are brothers, and we can trust one another."

During the following celebration, Jerusha came to Mark and said, "You kiss very well, Captain Edge."

Edge glared at her. "And *you* shut up, or I'll give you a sample!"

Jerusha's eyes opened wide, and for once she had nothing clever to say. "Don't you touch me!"

Edge grinned. "You're better-looking than Locor."

When he took a step forward, Jerusha turned and fled. The captain laughed, and the others, who had been watching, were laughing as well.

She sat on the floor with her back to the stone wall, her cheeks blazing. Edge came over to join her, and she watched him with apprehension. "Get away from me, Captain!"

"Don't worry. I just wanted to tell you that you did a good job." He sat down beside her. "You all did a good job. If it weren't for the Junior Space Rangers, none of this would have happened, and I want to thank you."

"Why—" Jerusha was almost speechless again. She swallowed and said, "You're welcome."

"If a kiss isn't all right, how about a handshake between shipmates?"

"I—I think that would be fine, Captain."

His hand closed around hers, and he said warmly, "You're a good shipmate, Jerusha Ericson. I've never had better!"

14
Attack!

Jerusha settled back on a couch in *Daystar* and smiled at Raina. "Well, we had a good visit with new people. I didn't think I'd like the inhabitants of Makon at all, but they're really rather nice, despite their savage appearance."

"They're people," Raina said simply. "Jesus died for them like He died for you or for me."

"That's right. We must never forget that."

Raina leaned forward and looked out the porthole as the planet Makon disappeared into the distance. "I wonder if we'll ever come back here again."

"You can be sure Captain Edge will. He's still got the idea of getting rich from tridium. And I must admit, I wouldn't mind having a little extra financial security myself." She laughed. "I don't know what I mean by *extra*. I never had any to begin with."

"No, I don't suppose any of us have ever had much money."

The girls were still talking quietly when Heck Jordan came in. As usual, he plumped himself down right between them. When they drew back, he said, "What's the matter? You two man-haters?"

"Not really." Raina smiled. "When you get to be a man, you'll find that out."

"Ah, come on," Heck said, flushing. "After all, I'm going to be rich."

"Are you, Heck?" Raina asked.

"We all are. About this tridium, I've been doing a

155

little figuring." He began to spiel out figures, enormous amounts of money. Then he leaned back expansively and said, "I may even buy myself a ship like the Intergalactic Rangers'—then I'll be the captain and give the orders."

"Remind me not to sign on." Jerusha said.

"Why? What would be wrong with having me for a captain?"

"Nothing—after you grow up." Jerusha got up and left.

Ringo Smith came by, saw Heck sitting with Raina, and turned to go.

But Raina called out, "Wait, Ringo! Come over and join us!"

Ringo hesitated, then entered the room and sat down. He looked down at his feet and listened as Heck spun tales of impossible riches.

"But money's not everything," Raina argued.

Heck spent the next five minutes trying to convince her that it was. Then he threw up his hands. "I give up. You're just too religious." Leaping to his feet, he went out of the room, calling, "Hey, Mei-Lani, let me tell you about the new spaceship I'm going to buy . . ."

"He's impossible." Raina laughed.

Then Ringo looked up and saw that she was smiling at him. "I guess so," he said. He took a deep breath and said, "Raina, I've got to tell you something."

"Why, of course, Ringo. What is it?"

Ringo had been rehearsing this speech, but now that it was time to give it he could not seem to find the words. He twisted his hands together, unable to meet Raina's clear green eyes. He ducked his head and stared again at his feet. Finally he mumbled, "I ran away and left you for the enemy, Raina."

Raina moved over and took Ringo's hand. "We've been over this before. It all happened so quickly. You didn't have time—"

"Yes, I did have time! I'm just a coward!"

"No, you're not a coward. You know how I know?"

"How?"

"If you were a coward, you would never have told me so. You would never have come in and apologized. It's harder for most people to apologize than it is to face a physical enemy."

She continued speaking softly, and Ringo started to relax. "Well," he said finally, very much aware of her soft hand holding his, "I don't exactly see it that way. But someday I hope to show you that I'm not quite the wimp that I seem."

"Wimp? What's a *wimp?*"

"Oh, that's what they used to call a nothing person back in the old days. Mei-Lani was telling me about it." He looked down at her hand and was about to say, "You're the prettiest girl I ever saw, Raina," but he was interrupted when Studs Cagney came through, whistling a tune.

Studs looked at them and started to say something, then seeing the expression on Ringo's face, shrugged his burly shoulders and passed on by the door.

Raina said, "Promise me something, will you, Ringo?"

"Anything!"

"All right. Now, remember you promised. I want you to forget what happened out there. It doesn't do us any good to dwell on what we think are our failures. I have plenty of my own. But although there's nothing to forgive, I want you to know I forgive you, and God will forgive you if you only ask. And if I forgive you and God forgives you, what's left to be ashamed about?"

Ringo looked up in surprise. He had admired the soft beauty of Raina St. Clair for a long time but had been put off by what he considered her strict religion. Now he saw a side of her that he had not seen before, a strength that he envied. He nodded and swallowed hard, then said, "All right. I'll stop thinking about it."

"Good. Now let's go to the galley and get something to drink."

The trip back to Earth was going smoothly, and the relaxed crew spent many hours improving the various computer and electronic systems aboard *Daystar*.

One day Bronwen announced over the ship's intercom, "We are coming into the vicinity of the Eagle Nebula. Junior Space Rangers report to the bridge."

One by one the Rangers entered the bridge, and each of them was awestruck at the size of the nebula.

Raina summed up what probably they were all feeling. "Somehow the tremendous size of the universe just doesn't register until you're flying next to one of these."

The Eagle Nebula consisted of three tall columns of gases resembling a great eagle. The tallest column was more than three light-years in height. The gases in the nebula were swirling clouds of dark brown and reddish orange. In some areas the gases formed into thick clumps. As these swirled about, sometimes bright white light would escape momentarily.

Bronwen explained. "In this nebula the condensing action of molecular hydrogen and dust form huge lumps that contract and, it's thought, finally ignite into stars. The gravity at work in a nebula of this size is unmeasurable to our science."

Heck said he could see some stars hidden inside

the thick clouds. "Will the stars always remain hidden?" he asked Bronwen.

"No, Heck. Sometime in years to come, the ultraviolet light produced by the other stars in this sector will evaporate the clouds. Then those stars will burst forth in their full radiance."

Feeling overwhelmed by the sight, Jerusha sat and whispered, "And the heavens shall praise thy wonders, O Lord . . ."

Standing next to Jerusha, Dai said, "That's beautiful. Where is it from?"

"It's from the Psalms. The Bible is full of passages about the wonders of God's creation." She smiled at him, then looked back at the Eagle Nebula. "I have no doubt we're looking at one now."

Pondering the Rangers' comments, Mark Edge thought, *I never really looked at it that way, but maybe there's really more to this universe than I think.*

Edge's crew had learned to work well together, and even Tara Jaleel seemed to have mellowed. Strangely, she spent much time with Bronwen Llewellen.

"I never know what those two have to say to each other," Dai said. "Jaleel is so different from my aunt."

"I think she admires your aunt a great deal. You know, *together* they make a perfect woman," Mei-Lani said.

"How's that?"

"I think I know." Zeno Thrax was sitting across from them. He looked at Mei-Lani and said, "You're thinking that Lieutenant Jaleel has strength and limitless courage, and Bronwen Llewellen has gentleness and enough love to load a spaceship."

"That's right, Zeno. Do you agree?"

"I do, indeed, but they are two women and not one." Then Thrax rose, saying, "Soon we'll be getting back into the earth's atmosphere."

The ship suddenly gave a mighty jolt, and the captain's voice screamed over the speaker, "Battle stations! Battle stations! Condition red!"

All three ran to the bridge, where they found Tara Jaleel rapidly directing the weapons fire.

Squeezing off rounds as quickly as her trigger finger could move, Jaleel shouted to Edge, "It looks like a Jackray class cruiser. She came up behind us when we passed Uranus."

Several turbo laser blasts struck *Daystar*.

"We can't outgun them, that's for sure. A few more hits and our deflector will be gone." Edge dodged and wove and finally brought *Daystar* into the vicinity of Mars. "Tara, I'm going to swing around Mars and make them think we're landing. Once our position is behind Mars, we'll swing out to the asteroid Vesta and hide in a cave I know about."

Edge smoothly piloted *Daystar* around Mars, then bolted toward Vesta. The Jackray cruiser was many times larger than *Daystar* and would have to slow her speed upon approaching the asteroid belt.

"Edge to Crew. Secure yourselves. It's going to get bumpy in there."

Daystar glided into the cave opening, still smoking from the shellacking she just received from the Jackray.

"Petroski to Edge." The urgent voice of the engineer sounded over the intercom.

"Go ahead, Ivan."

"Captain, what in Saturn's name is going on? Who's firing on us?"

Before Edge could answer, Bronwen interrupted. "Captain, we only have a few minutes in here after all. That cruiser is pulling away from Mars and heading in our direction."

Edge ordered, "Everyone hold onto your hats. I'll make an attempt to outrun them back to Earth. There's got to be a couple of Intergalactic cruisers roaming near Earth somewhere. If they see the Jackray firing on us, they'll intercept her."

The Mark V Star Drive engines blasted *Daystar* out of the cave and toward the blue-green planet. The Jackray was after them immediately. Edge kept dodging and weaving his ship so that the enemy's weapons could not get a direct hit. Then the cruiser stopped firing turbo lasers and launched a volley from her neutron cannons. The effect was devastating.

"Engineering to Captain." Ivan's voice was frantic. "We've got to land her. The shields are gone. We've lost engineering control to the engines, and I have to power them down at once!" There was a pause on the intercom, then Petroski continued. "Catastrophic shutdown will occur in six minutes."

Keeping a tight rein on his emotions, Edge calculated they were headed straight for Earth. If his luck held, he would need to use only his thrusters and not the main engines. "Shut 'em down, Ivan, but keep thruster power at maximum."

Glancing at the rear view screen, Edge thought, *Why doesn't she finish us? They have a clear shot!*

Zeno Thrax interrupted his thoughts. "Captain, they've opened a channel and demand to speak to you."

"Put it on the comm," Edge replied. "Maybe this will give us some time."

"Surrender, or we'll blow you out of the sky!"

"I know *that* voice," Captain Edge said, his lips drawn together so tightly they were white.

"It's Sir Richard Irons, isn't it?" Jerusha whispered.

"Yes, and he'll have the location of Makon out of us or kill us all." The captain barked an order at Jaleel. "Keep firing—give 'em all we've got."

The Jackray cruiser gained on *Daystar.* Edge surmised their strategy and said to the bridge crew, "They don't want to finish us off just yet. Irons wants Makon's location. He'll tractor us any moment."

Suddenly, when all hope appeared lost for *Daystar,* the Jackray inexplicably turned and rocketed away at top speed.

"What happened to *them?*" Raina asked.

Then the *Daystar* began to bounce and pitch, yawing from side to side. Edge breathed anxiously. "They must have seen something." For some reason he guessed that Raina had been praying, and he said to her, "This would be a good time to continue your prayer."

Daystar plummeted toward Earth. The atmosphere around the ship's surface turned bright red. Sparks flew off the spacecraft in every direction. Portions of the wing surfaces began to peel away due to the extreme heat.

Bronwen calmly called to the captain. "Use the thrusters, Captain. You can soft-land her in the Great Indian Desert. It's just ten degrees starboard from our heading."

Edge made the necessary adjustment to the heading and lifted the craft's nose with the forward stabilizer. *Thank goodness Jerusha thought to triple-coat the stabilizers,* he thought, *or we'd be dead meat!*

He brought *Daystar* parallel to the desert floor and soft-landed her on her belly. Even so, the set-down jolted the crew to the bone. Fragments of wing flew in all directions. The nose section sheared apart in three separate pieces. After sliding through the hot sand of the barren desert for almost two miles, what was left of *Daystar* finally came to rest.

And there wasn't so much as one computer chip left aboard the ship!

15

A New Commission

Captain Edge walked around the *Daystar*, his face grim, closely followed by Ivan Petroski and Zeno Thrax. The three men studied the battle damage.

Then Edge asked, "What do you think? Will she ever fly again?" He knew Thrax's mind had been working. Zeno would have assessed the damage quickly.

"It'll fly, but it'll cost a lot of money to get it in shape again."

Ivan Petroski nodded in agreement. "The first officer's right, Captain. We've taken a lot of damage. Almost all of the computer system will have to be replaced. Electronics is shot. There's lots of structural damage, and I don't know about the Star Drive yet."

The three men stood by the spaceship for a while, looking glum. When there seemed to be nothing else to say, Edge turned and walked off.

He found the youngest members of his crew waiting for him, but no one was more glad to see him than Contessa. As usual, she put her paws on his chest and tried to lick his face.

"Ericson, get this animal off me!"

Jerusha whispered, "Contessa!" and when the dog came, she said quietly, "I'm sorry, Captain. She just likes you so much."

"What do you think, Captain?" Heck Jordan asked worriedly. He glanced over at the ship. "It's going to take an electronics genius like me to put the electronic system back in shape. But I'm gonna need lots of parts, and—"

Ringo broke in. "And the computer subsystems are just about ruined. The main computer may be all right—I won't know until I look at it—but we're in real trouble, Captain."

Captain Edge's face was dark with worry.

Raina said gently, "We'll stay with you, Captain Edge."

"Yes, we will." Bronwen Llewellen joined the group. "And I won't say anything in Welsh this time. That wasn't fair." Her smile was gentle, and for the first time she put a hand on Edge's arm, saying, "You will fly again."

Edge stared at her. "Did God tell you that?" But his tone was not antagonistic, as it had once been.

"No, not directly," Bronwen said. "But I've lived a long time, Captain. I know that something has happened to you in the past few weeks. You're not the same man you were when we left Earth."

"That's very true," Mei-Lani said, smiling at him, too. "The man who left here would not have been accepted by Chief Locor. The chief is a very wise and perceptive man."

One after another of the young crew members encouraged the captain until he threw up his hands and said, "All right. All right! I'm convinced!" Then he considered the next step. "We've got some samples of tridium. I'll have to go try to sell someone on the idea of speculating."

"You'll do it, Captain," Jerusha said.

"If I can get out of here to civilization, that is."

"You know what *I* think?" Dai Bando said. Dai so rarely spoke up in groups that everyone looked at him.

"What do you think, Dai?" Raina smiled.

"I think we ought to have a victory celebration first of all."

"Hey, that's a good idea! I'm glad I thought of it." Heck grinned. "Let's go find some fancy banquet hall and order the best they've got."

"In the desert?"

A laugh went up, but everybody seemed to feel better.

"Someone's coming," Ringo said, before the captain, Bronwen, or any of the Junior Space Rangers could move.

As it happened, Ringo Smith did have one talent beside understanding computers. He was scarcely aware of it himself, but his senses were highly developed. He could hear better and see farther than anyone else on the crew.

Edge said with a puzzled frown, "I don't see anything."

"But don't you hear it? It's a ship—coming from that direction." Ringo was pleased that he could at least do *something* better than Dai Bando. "It's far off, but it's headed this way."

"It may be Irons coming back," Captain Edge said. "We'd better get our weapons turned."

"No, it's not the same ship, sir. Look, there it is."

They all looked.

Zeno asked in astonishment, "Can you see something? I can't see *anything!*"

"Right over the horizon—there!" Ringo said. He squinted. "It's an official ship of the Intergalactic Council!"

"Then it can't be Irons—unless he's taken over," Captain Edge said. "That must be what scared him off." Then he listened hard and stared for a while. "There it

167

is. I can see just a flash." He turned to Ringo. "Why didn't you tell me you could see that far and hear that well? I would have made you chief lookout."

Ringo flushed. "I don't know," he said. "I don't think much about it."

Raina nudged him with her shoulder. "I didn't know you could do it either. It must be wonderful to be able to see that far and hear that well."

"Well, that's not all," Ringo said as the others scanned the horizon. "I can smell better than most people, too. As a matter of fact, that perfume you wear—I can smell it half a mile away."

"It's not *that* strong, or is it? Maybe it's too strong."

"No," Ringo said quickly, "it's not. I like it. It's just that . . . well . . ." He ran out of words then, but it was just as well, for the ship was now plainly visible.

"What's the insignia? Can you see it, Ringo?" Captain Edge asked.

Ringo took one glance. "It's got a star on it—a star inside a square."

He did not know what that meant, but both Zeno Thrax and Captain Edge gasped. "It's the commandant's personal ship! Commandant Winona Lee!"

They had all heard of Commandant Winona Lee. She was, without a doubt, one of the most powerful leaders in the Intergalactic Confederation.

"What is she doing here?"

"I don't know, but she's a powerful woman," Zeno Thrax said. "We may be in trouble."

"Any of you take anything when you left the Academy?" Edge asked worriedly. When they all shook their heads, he said, "Then, it may be me she's after. Irons is a powerful man. He may have convinced the commandant that I'm nothing but a thief." He straightened up and said, "Well, I'll keep all of you out of it. After all, you didn't have anything to do with this."

"We were all in it together, Captain Edge," Jerusha said loyally.

"That's right" . . . "We're all in it" . . . "Yes, we're with you." The words came from the Junior Space Rangers.

Edge looked around at them and said, "Well, you're a bunch of fine young men and women." At that instant two paws struck him in the back and knocked him to his knees in the sand. He had to fight Contessa off. He got to his feet, stared down at his dusty uniform, and said, "A fine way to meet the commandant of the Intergalactic Council. Thanks a lot, Contessa!"

Contessa would have gone to him again, but Jerusha said, "No! You're a naughty dog! Stay here! Sit!"

The commandant's ship came for a smooth landing, and the crew of the *Daystar* lined up in military formation and at attention. Captain Edge and First Officer Zeno Thrax stood in front of the line.

The doors slid open with a hiss, and a woman in her late forties stepped down. She was not a beautiful woman and not particularly noticeable, yet there was something about her that bespoke the authority of her office. She came directly to the two men.

"Captain, I'm glad to find you."

Edge bowed deeply, as did Thrax and the rest of the crew. "I apologize for my appearance—"

"It doesn't matter. I can see you have had problems with your spacecraft. Come aboard my ship." She looked over his ragtag crew, and a smile touched her lips. "I seem to recognize some of your people. We'll have them aboard, too." She turned to the tall man who had followed her. "Captain Pursey, see that the *Day-*

star crew is entertained while the captain and his first officer come with me."

What followed was remarkable. The entire crew was led into the commandant's large spaceship. They were served food that was real food. Heck ate so fast he could hardly talk. The others, tired of the poor fare on Makon and on the *Daystar* itself, were equally hungry.

The meal was not yet over when Captain Pursey reappeared and said, "Ensign Ericson, would you bring your people—the Junior Space Rangers, I think you call yourselves. The commandant requires your presence."

The ensigns followed Captain Pursey down immaculate, shining corridors to the medium-sized room where Commandant Winona Lee sat at a table. They lined up in front of her.

Jerusha noted that Captain Edge and Zeno Thrax sat at the far end of the table. She also sensed strong emotions in the air, but they were not *bad*, she thought. She kept studying the face of the commandant, trying to guess what was coming.

Commandant Lee said, "I have been aware of the activities of your captain for some time." She turned her head, and her sharp eyes picked out Edge, who flushed. "Unfortunately, some of his activities have not been entirely legal."

By the time she was through, the captain was practically wilted.

I bet he's never had a put-down like that, Jerusha thought. And then another thought popped into her mind: *But it's been good for the captain. He has needed something like this for a long time. Now that he's had it, he'll be a better man.*

She turned her attention back to the commandant, who stood to her feet suddenly. "I need your help," she said abruptly to the Space Rangers. "That surprises you. And you would probably ask, 'What would the commandant of the Intergalactic Council possibly need with another ship or with another crew?'" She stroked her chin thoughtfully. She had beautiful gray hair, her best feature, and she touched it in womanly fashion.

"I do need your help, for I need a ship to send on missions that are too—" she paused "—too *delicate*, shall we say, for authorized ships of the Intergalactic Fleet." She let her words sink in, smiling at the shock on their faces. "I want you young people to become my own special force. You will be called the *Daystar* Rangers, and you will be sent to spots in the galaxy that are potentially dangerous. I must warn you that it will not be easy. There may be times when you will hate me for sending you to some of these places." She bowed her head, and Jerusha saw the weight that was on her from the tremendous pressures of her job.

When the commandant raised her head, her smile was gone, and she was very serious. "You will be well paid, and those of you who have done wrong in the past will not be called to account for your mistakes. And now you will talk it over and give me your answer. Yes or no?"

Captain Edge stood back and watched the ensigns as they battled back and forth. Heck Jordan was totally opposed to accepting Commander Lee's offer. He said loudly, "Well paid? What does that mean? I say we go back to Makon and make a million! What do you say, Captain?"

Edge shook his head. "This is a decision for you young people. I think she sees you as a potential scouting force to go to places where she wouldn't dare send

171

an ordinary fleet. As she says, it will be dangerous. But you decide."

The argument went on and on until Jerusha said, "I think we should take her offer, and I think we should take a vote. Majority rules."

The vote went as Edge had sensed. Only Heck was against it, and even he gave in when he saw the way the wind was blowing. "Yes, it may be a good political maneuver," he said. "I can get close to the chairman. You've got to know the right people to get on in this part of the galaxy."

"Be quiet, Heck," Raina snapped. She looked up at Edge and said, "Well, Captain, you have our answer."

"All of you are in favor, then?" Edge turned to Jerusha, and she smiled. "Are you willing to fly with a rough captain like me? The commandant didn't tell you, but if you agree, she's going to refit the *Daystar*. I would be in command of the ship."

"We're all in favor, Captain Edge!"

"Very well. Let's go see the commandant."

Soon they were assembled in front of Commandant Lee, and she said, "What is your decision?"

Jerusha was the spokesman. "We appreciate your confidence, Commandant Lee, and we will do the best we possibly can for you. I pledge my personal allegiance to you."

One by one the young people did the same, while Edge watched.

Commandant Lee said, "I appreciate this. The *Daystar* Rangers will be a source of pride to me personally and to the entire Council. Much of what you do will be secret. You will get no thanks for it. As a matter of fact, sometimes you may even be persecuted for it, but you will have the thanks of a very grateful woman. Now," she said, "already I have a mission in mind for you . . ."

172

When the commandant had finished outlining their assignment, she dismissed them, saying, "We will be taking you into the capital while your ship is being refitted. We will get you special uniforms, you will be taught weaponry, the latest in electronics and computers. You will also be taught the history of your galaxy." She lowered her head. "And I pray that God would be with you all."

As Jerusha walked from the cabin, she found Mark Edge at her side. She looked up and said suddenly with a pixieish smile, "So you're going to be an honest man instead of a pirate?"

Captain Edge reached out, took her hand, and held it as he once had. "I'll have to, Jerusha," he said. "You'll be breathing down my neck, reading my mind. That's a lot for a man to put up with. I don't know what—"

Something heavy struck him on the shoulders and knocked him against Jerusha. Off balance, she fell backward, and he went down with her. They both struggled to get up, while Contessa barked short, happy barks and licked Captain Edge's face.

Edge shoved the animal away with one hand while still holding Jerusha's hand with the other. "Can't you do *anything* with this animal?"

Jerusha laughed. "You have an irresistible charm. She can't stay away from you."

Edge squeezed her hand as they got to their feet. "Well, I'm glad to hear that. Now, when you grow up . . ."

Jerusha flushed. She said, "Let's go, Captain Edge. I don't want to hear any more about this."

The two continued down the corridor, laughing. Contessa still pushed against Edge, who protested that he could never learn to love dogs.

Jerusha turned to him. "You can do anything you want to, Captain Mark Edge."

Edge found this interesting. "You really think that? Then I'll tell you a secret."

"What is it, Captain?"

He said in a loud whisper, "I think the same about you, Ensign."

Color touched Jerusha Ericson's face. "Come along, Captain. Let's go get started on this new mission."

Get swept away in the many Gilbert Morris Adventures available from Moody Press:

"Too Smart" Jones

4025-8 Pool Party Thief
4026-6 Buried Jewels
4027-4 Disappearing Dogs
4028-2 Dangerous Woman
4029-0 Stranger in the Cave
4030-4 Cat's Secret
4031-2 Stolen Bicycle
4032-0 Wilderness Mystery
4033-9 Spooky Mansion
4034-7 Mysterious Artist

Come along for the adventures and mysteries Juliet "Too Smart" Jones always manages to find. She and her other homeschool friends solve these great adventures and learn biblical truths along the way. Ages 9-14

Seven Sleepers - The Lost Chronicles

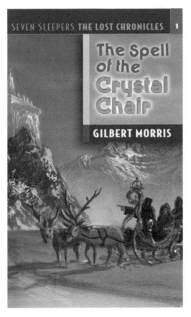

3667-6 The Spell of the Crystal Chair
3668-4 The Savage Game of Lord Zarak
3669-2 The Strange Creatures of Dr. Korbo
3670-6 City of the Cyborgs
3671-4 The Temptations of Pleasure Island
3672-2 Victims of Nimbo
3673-0 The Terrible Beast of Zor

More exciting adventures from the Seven Sleepers. As these exciting young people attempt to faithfully follow Goél, they learn important moral and spiritual lessons. Come along with them as they encounter danger, intrigue, and mystery. Ages 10-14

Dixie Morris Animal Adventures

3363-4 Dixie and Jumbo
3364-2 Dixie and Stripes
3365-0 Dixie and Dolly
3366-9 Dixie and Sandy
3367-7 Dixie and Ivan
3368-5 Dixie and Bandit
3369-3 Dixie and Champ
3370-7 Dixie and Perry
3371-5 Dixie and Blizzard
3382-3 Dixie and Flash

Follow the exciting adventures of this animal lover as she learns more of God and His character through her many adventures underneath the Big Top.
Ages 9-14

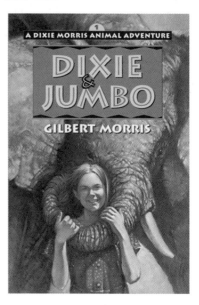

The Daystar Voyages

4102-X Secret of the Planet Makon
4106-8 Wizards of the Galaxy
4107-6 Escape From the Red Comet
4108-4 Dark Spell Over Morlandria
4109-2 Revenge of the Space Pirates
4110-6 Invasion of the Killer Locusts
4111-4 Dangers of the Rainbow Nebula
4112-2 The Frozen Space Pilot
4113-0 White Dragon of Sharnu
4114-9 Attack of the Denebian Starship

Join the crew of the Daystar as they traverse the wide expanse of space. Adventure and danger abound, but they learn time and again that God is truly the Master of the Universe.
Ages 10-14

MOODY
The Name You Can Trust
1-800-678-8812 www.MoodyPress.org